THE DEAD OF WINTER

D. Thompson

86/3

D0838590

ff

THE DEAD
OF WINTER

Dominic
Cooper

faber and faber

LONDON · BOSTON

First published in 1975
by Chatto and Windus Limited, London
First published in this edition in 1985
by Faber and Faber Limited
3 Queen Square London WC1N 3AU

Printed in Great Britain by
Whitstable Litho Ltd., Whitstable, Kent
All rights reserved

© Dominic Cooper, 1975

*This book is sold subject to the condition that it shall not,
by way of trade or otherwise, be lent, re-sold, hired out
or otherwise circulated without the publisher's prior consent
in any form of binding or cover other than that in which
it is published and without a similar condition including this
condition being imposed on the subsequent purchaser*

British Library Cataloguing in Publication Data

Cooper, Dominic
The dead of winter.
I. Title
823'.914 [F]   PR6053.O546/

ISBN 0-571-13601-X

For
Sylvia

Annan dag eftir býr hann ferð sína til skips ok sagði þá öllu liði, at hann myndi ríða í braut alfari, ok þótti mönnum þat mikit, en væntu þó tilkvámu hans síðar. Gunnarr hverfr til allra manna, er hann var búinn. Gengu menn út með honum allir. Hann stingr niðr atgeirinum ok stiklar í söðulinn, ok ríða þeir Kolskeggr í braut. Þeir ríða fram at Markarfljóti. Þá drap hestr Gunnars fæti ok stökk hann af baki. Honum varð litit upp til hlíðarinnar ok bæjarins at Hlíðarenda ok mælti: 'Fögr er hlíðin, svá at mér hefir hon aldri jafnfögr sýnzt, bleikir akrar, en slegin tún, ok mun ek ríða heim aftr ok fara hvergi.' 'Ger þú eigi þann óvina fagnað,' segir Kolskeggr, 'at þú rjúfir sætt þína, því at þér myndi engi maðr þat ætla, ok munt þú þat ætla mega, at svá mun allt fara sem Njáll hefir sagt.' 'Hvergi mun ek fara,' segir Gunnarr, 'ok svá vilda ek, at þú gerðir.'

NJÁLS SAGA, *Islendinga Sögur XI*

Early next morning he made ready to ride to the ship, and told all his people that he was going abroad for ever. Everyone was dismayed at the news, but hoped that some day he would return. When he was ready to leave, he embraced them all one by one. The whole household came out to see him off. With a thrust of his halberd he vaulted into the saddle, and rode away with Kolskegg.

They rode down towards Markar River. Just then Gunnar's horse stumbled, and he had to leap from the saddle. He happened to glance up towards his home and the slopes of Hlidarend.

'How lovely the slopes are,' he said, 'more lovely than they have ever seemed to me before, golden cornfields and new-mown hay. I am going back home, and I will not go away.'

Kolskegg said, 'Do not make your enemies happy by breaking the settlement, something that no one would ever expect of you. For you can be quite sure that all of Njal's predictions will come true.'

'I am not going away,' said Gunnar. 'And I wish you would stay too.'

NJÁLS SAGA, *trans. Magnús Magnússon and Hermann Pálsson*

1

THE sun. And what had been an immense, dimensionless gun-barrel of heat earlier that autumn day was now a tamed power casting a layer of brass over the plains of the Atlantic. The flickering light came ceaselessly across the sea, mile upon mile of it, gained the rocks and skerries of the coast, slipped up and across the raised beaches, powered its way up the final hundred and fifty feet of the cliff where the grass and dwarf birches lay beaten down against the surface of the earth and then sank itself into the hillsides of heather and peat-moss which stretched in terraces and gentle slopes backwards into the blue sky over the island. A faint breeze carried the smell of bog-myrtle and heather and sea-life. All along the coast of the great bare headland the same thing was happening so that the whole mass of land which stood, with its flattened, rounded end, out into the ocean was trembling with warmth and life, calmed by the final weeks of a long summer before the winter, inevitable, arrived with its winds and rain.

Alasdair Mór, too, felt the sun and trembled as he walked. The water rose from the peat-moss, all yellow and green and brown wetness, under the

weight of his tackety boots and he moved seawards on to drier ground. Once he was on this
firmer footing his great body settled into its
steady, shambling gait. He moved like a bear on its
hindlegs, with small steps and his sloping
shoulders slightly in advance of the rest of him,
hands dangling like forepaws; chest, waist and
hips rolling clumsily. He felt his thighs tautening
beneath the coarse-woven trousers as he worked
his way up a rise and through a patch of knee-deep
heathers. His thick sweater, oiled grey-green wool,
and his stained and tattered leather jerkin, both
seasons old, all contrived to constrict him as he
moved upwards. He grunted twice to voice his
effort and then, with a final stride, was out on top
of a smooth green mound on the edge of the cliffs.
He paused. He shifted his greasy cap once, twice,
scratched the back of his neck and then, removing
his cap, bared his head to the sun.

His face was like his body, like the hillside
behind him. Rough, weather-beaten, heavy-boned.
A good-sized nose and ears and full, generous lips
like the flesh in the spocks of a grown crab. And
all over, with no regular pattern, there sprouted
little growths of hair. There was the stubble of an
unshaven face like the after-grass in an autumn
hay-field but there were also long, single hairs,
double hairs, clusters, that had never felt the
blade, which grew from the lobes of his ears, from
the end of his nose, from inside his nostrils, from
the thick ridges of his cheek-bones. His eyebrows

bushed and met in a great junction of pines above
his nose. The hair of his head was greasy and thick,
skart-black with no trace of grey that might have
come with his forty-five years. It rolled and
curled in a cold surf of disorder, wirily strong as
heather roots in his thick skull, only indented by
the mark of his cap's rim.

His face was contorted—his eyes narrowed, his
mouth stretched—as if the light were too strong.
But this was not the case. He had that way of
freezing his face in a grin when he was thinking.
And now, with the early October sun low over the
horizon, he was looking out to sea, slightly to the
north, where the swell rose and fell round the
rocks of Maisgeir. The weather would hold and he
was thinking. Thinking that it would be calm
enough to try some creels at the southern tip of
the skerry where the swell was least. He remembered the first time his father had taken him out to
Maisgeir. A similar day. He had been about nine.
He saw his father in the bows of their boat, himself at the oars holding the boat as stationary as
possible. His father, a large man, his heel wedged
under the gunwale for support, hauling the line
in hand over hand and the three creels slowly
appearing out of the water one after the other and
his own delight and his father's satisfaction at the
eight lobsters trapped in them. And him, forgetting his first man's responsibilities, jumping up
in the boat to examine the creatures and his
father, in a moment's anger and fear, barking at

him to be seated. The waters of Maisgeir were never to be taken so lightly. And how he blushed and accepted this just rebuke and how his father had later smiled again and them rowing back in the failing light, both silent but with something unspoken between them.

His father had been a lobster-fisherman all his life and Alasdair, from the age of thirteen, had followed him in the same trade. Before this he had dutifully attended the village school, some nine miles away, until his father had fallen and hurt his back. Then Mr Morrison, the schoolmaster from Aberdeen, had taken him aside one spring morning and told him that if his father needed help with the lobsters he could stop coming to school. Alasdair had waited silently, showing no re-action, while Mr Morrison explained that he would continue to tick his name on the register for the final months before the law allowed him to leave. Then he had just nodded and walked away and never set foot in the classroom again. The freedom from school where Ina Maclean and Jennie MacFadyen and Wee Jamie had tortured him with their taunts at his slow-moving mind had given him added strength as he learned to handle the heavy oars and the weights of the submerged creels. Four years later, when his father was more or less bed-ridden with the pains, his younger brother David had started coming out with him in the boat. For three years more the two sons had shared their time between fishing and looking after their helpless father. Their mother had died giving birth to David those many years back and there were few people within reach who could have come to lend a hand.

Then, quite suddenly, on a bright May morning, Alasdair had come back up from the shore to ask his father if he would like to be taken out into the sunshine. And his father had just lain there with his mouth wide open as if in the middle of a yawn, and his eyes staring at him in the doorway. For a moment Alasdair had not understood and then he had realised with a dull sense of loss and called David. And together they had tidied and washed him and then made a rare excursion into the small town to see the minister and Duncan the Hammer who would be the man to make up a rough coffin. And the next day they had walked over to Achateny to borrow a horse and cart and gone to collect the big, resonant coffin of unweathered wood. But Duncan had not seen their father for three summers or more and had not realised how he had wasted and shrunk in his invalid state so that when Alasdair and David came to lower the corpse into the coffin they saw that it was far too big. He, their big father, afraid of nothing, lay wizened and lost in the box. So they had packed some old fish sacks around him for fear that he would be knocked around on the journey into the town. And it seemed better to them that the odd smell of cold flesh was covered by the homely smells of dogfish and mackerel. Then they both shaved and splashed their hands and faces in the burn and loading the coffin on to the cart they drove in to the kirk, sitting side by side in shy silence on the driver's bench. A year later David had said goodbye and disappeared over the hill to find a new life.

Twenty-four years ago last January.

Five winters later, a letter had come from a town in Canada to tell that he was married with a small son. Alasdair had read the letter with difficulty sitting on a rock outside the croft and had glanced up at the sea's horizon knowing dimly that Canada lay out over that way.

Alasdair bent down and picked up a piece of rock the size of a sheep's eyeball. His great hands closed softly over the lump, caressing it, feeling out its shape, letting the warmth creep into his skin, finding pleasure and security in a sharp edge, a flattened side. The years since his brother's departure stretched behind him in a belt of time in which there were few landmarks beyond the recurring seasons. But he was only aware of the length of his life alone when he began to think of David and his old father. And even in the first months after David had left when a prolonged winter had kept him off the sea and reduced him to chewing the sour, raw berries of the rowan tree, even then it had never occurred to him to follow David's example and leave home in search of an easier life. He squeezed the rock. This was his land, his sea. These he knew. . . . At the back of the headland where the road passed he was already beginning to feel the nearness of other people so that when he returned from one of his meetings at the road-end with Aulay, the old shepherd from Achateny, who brought him his supplies from the town, he walked faster than usual, always glancing up to catch the first sight of his croft.

His thinking face relaxed showing the slight cast in his right-hand eye. It was this which had led Ina and Jennie and Wee Jamie and later other people to treat him as a half-wit for the slowness of his face with this misalignment of his eyes gave him the look of unworldly incomprehension. And yet there was no malice, no wilfulness in his looks; just a detachment, an isolation which had made the other children uncertain of him so that they, in their fear, had attacked him pitilessly.

But he ought to be moving on if the creels were to be set before dark and with a snuff of his nose he rolled off along the cliff. Down below him lay the two tiers of raised beaches where his grandfather's people had grown the barley for their whisky. Great green steps between the brown hills and the hyaline sea, they now lay unworked, the furrows in the grass fast disappearing beneath the proliferating bracken. Here the Achateny sheep grazed, furry lice scattered along the coast, their pathetic cries mingling with the mad threats of the black-backs, herring gulls and hoodies which plunged and climbed and wheeled over the shoreland. Beyond, the great castling rocks stood black by the sea and tongues and skerries prickled in among light surf as the tide rose over them.

A few yards further on Alasdair turned down a narrow gullet in the cliff where a steep, zig-zagging track led down to the natural harbour of Port nam Freumh. The track was dusty and loose after the warm weeks of the summer and he slipped and slithered as he hurried on. Over the first beach, down another small track to the left, across the second beach, along the dry bulk of a long rock protruding into the sea as a jetty and he was by his boat.

The boat–his father's before him–lay in the shadow thrown by the jetty and the sea-fortress rock out at the end. It was heavy, clinker-built, with a raised elongated prow. Here, where nothing but the wildest seas could reach, it hung passively in a fathom of water the colour of colourless glass whose very stillness in the shadows seemed arctic cold. Out beyond the shadows, the surface of the water shimmered and breathed off metallic vapours of light and life. And this was the mystery of the sea.

He worked quickly collecting the creels and little rusty buoys and the cork floats and lines and then filled an old box with bait from a barrel that stood by the water's edge.

At last he was done and clutching the box of

bait he dropped like a goat into the bows of the
boat. He slipped the mooring rope and pushed the
boat away from the rock. For the few seconds
while he waited for room to use the oars the boat
swung over the freezing depths like a fantastic
prison ship, the hulks, with its tower of tarred
cages. And then with the first two pulls on the oars
its forward end issued out into the sunlight and
the movement of the unlocked sea so that the old
wood and then Alasdair and finally the creels all
shone and sparkled with the reflected sun darting
at every glossy or polished point.

The sun on your back is a good way to row. So
it seemed to Alasdair as he dropped his shoulders
forward and then straightened his back again in
an ancient, instinctive rhythm and the sea slipped
its oiled limbs beneath the wood and vanished in a
trail of bubbles and swirls astern.

When he had rowed up the coast, he turned the
boat round and sidled in closer to the shore. He
baited each of three creels that were attached to
the same line, fixing the glutinous gobbets of fish
next to the stone weights. Then, choosing a good
spot near the off-shore rocks, he carefully fed the
primed sea-traps over the gunwale. The wavering
shapes disappeared quickly into the waters until
all that showed was the rusty buoy, the top float
and a length of line bowing away into nothingness.

The oars lay down in the water, moving with
the gentle shifting of the sea and Alasdair heard
the pitchless grinding of the wooden thole-pins

and was pleased. How often had this happened before in his life? How often would it come again? The great cliffs rose above him with their gullets and landslides and patchy, pubic growths of birch and hazel and rowan. He glanced up and saw way down the coast, his path home lying like a discarded length of rope on the slope.

At strategic points all down the coast he set his creels. Then he turned the boat out to sea and bent his back into the oars. He heard the water bumping under the bows behind him, saw a strand of kelp pass by and then the bubbling wake and knew that he was making good speed. His breath sang in his nostrils, odd unpredictable gruntings rose from his throat and his eyes darted around him ceaselessly, the cast in his eye allowing him to see things which other men could never see. Behind him grew the suckings and slappings of the swell as he closed in on Maisgeir.

The skerry was, in fact, a small island at its southernmost end for in the area of a few square yards it rose to the height of fifteen feet or more above high water. There thin clumps of grass grew among the cast-up tangle and the empty crab shells left by the feeding birds. But northwards of this the level of the rock lay sunken beneath the sea at anything but low water and its arms and ledges and spines caught wind and current so that a turbulent swell and surf were always present.

With easy skill, Alasdair ran the boat in on the

swell, tossed a set of creels overboard and had turned the boat away again before the following wave could carry him on to the rocks. A few more powerful strokes took the boat clear into calmer water.

By now the sun was low, a fiery bubble of gas threatening to plunge into distant waters. Beyond Maisgeir the sea was an immense gilded haugh growing out on both sides of the river of fire, the sun's reflection. The skerry itself stood against this as a two-dimensional stain, no more than a hole in the exploding light, with sketches of surf playing around it, encasing it as the first fleece on a lamb.

Alasdair dropped the oars. He spat on the palm of each hand, rubbed them together thoughtfully, grasped the oars again and set off at a fast pace for the coast. He was wondering how long this autumn weather would hold. . . .

The boat which came round once a week and collected whatever lobsters he had, stopped in the winter months and he had to ask Aulay or one of the others at Achateny to take his catch into the town and sell it. Sometimes Aulay would come back obviously pleased with himself and hand over the few shillings with a look of personal triumph as though he had caught the lobsters himself. Alasdair smiled. Aulay had been telling him about the newcomer who had taken over the croft to the south of Rudha na Leap and started on the lobsters. Nobody seemed to know his

name but they called him An Sionnach, the Fox.
Aulay had said that it was not so much his reddy,
fair hair that had earned him his name as his
mysterious past and his slightly devious ways.
He didne speak hellish much, said Aulay, but
there was many a thought in yon skull of his. Och,
ye couldne know what he was after when ye were
talking to him. Aye, yon's a queer one. He's no
canny. He was away over the day to get some
twine from Erchie and ye should ha' heard the
way he was after getting yon for nothing. But
Erchie was having none of it and told the man the
twine was a penny an ounce, take it or leave it. . . .
Alasdair had not seen An Sionnach but even
those who had seemed unable to say anything
definite about him. Some said he was from the
Long Island, others that he came originally from
the Orkneys of Faroese parentage. All that could
be said for sure was that he had arrived with his
woman and a few belongings at the last moon.
And few people had even set eyes on her. It was
only Aulay and one of the other shepherds who
had seen her at a distance from the hills for she
had not yet been seen to leave the croft.

The men on the collection boat had said that
An Sionnach was doing well enough on the
lobsters. In spite of his pleas of poverty he appeared to be working with a newish boat and brand
new creels and lines, though where the money for
them had come from nobody knew. But these
men, too, felt uneasy with him – feared the silence

when his gaze bored into them. So that if they ever spoke of him they tried to joke about his strange ways, feeling that they could ward off the evil by not taking it seriously.

The boat slid onwards towards the shore, cuffing through the rippling waters, bending over the polished backs of the swell. Maisgeir and the horizon bobbed and bounced in the distance. Only Alasdair and the sun stood still.

Once back near the coast Alasdair laid some more creels just to the north of Port nam Freumh and then finished his work by setting his two last lines at the mouth of the burn whose waters, up at the back of the cliff, ran past his croft. Here he could always be sure of a good catch, for the lobsters came to feed off what the burn brought down from the hills.

And when the last creels were down and the boat seemed as vast and empty as a grain hopper, Alasdair breathed deeply and ran his hands over his thick hair. The day's work was done. And not too soon either. For the great sun was down in the sea, sliced in half like a fruit by the stroke of the horizon. And now the sea was no longer brassy but a carnage of bloody juices lying, like oil, on the old waters below, while the shadowy places, formerly glassy greens and dark blues from the light of the sky, now lay black and tarry.

For Alasdair, the sight of the dying sun splattering the world with its spurting flood was one of warmth and promise. It meant that the day was done with, that he knew nothing but happiness in that he had completed what he had set out to do earlier that day, that he could now return to his croft and animals and while away the evening hours in small matters, watching the life of a meagre fire and knowing that the stars and moon were rising over a still sea. So, for the last time that day, he bent his back and settled the callouses of his hands squarely on the smoothness of the oars and the boat leapt forward up the coast until its prow slotted itself into the black hole of Port nam Freumh. There he shipped the oars, tied up and unloaded a few odds and ends. Then he took one deep sighting of the sea, opened the barrel and, nostrils and eyes a-quiver, drew the old sweetness of his dead fish into his stomach, closed the barrel and turned for the path. Alasdair Mór was on his way home.

2

I T was only the birds climbing on the thermal
currents near the cliffs that ever got an all-
encompassing view of Cragaig in relationship to
the surrounding countryside. For the village lay,
facing southwestwards, in a small green hollow
behind the cliffs. And where there might have been
a few yards of grass between the houses and the
plunging cliff there was in fact a large hillock, an
escarpment, covered with deep, sprung heathers
which, with the surrounding hills behind, made
Cragaig a hidden, wondrous place. For here on this
small patch of cropped green grass set among
many hundreds of acres of rough land, the sunlight fell with a dazzling brightness which seemed
to make the earth glow with warmth and life.
Hidden, as it was, from sight from both land and
sea, this grassy corner lay with a certain primeval
purity as if the hills about it had been as a gangue
to its solitary existence over the years. There
had always been a secrecy, a sensation of collusion
between the place and those who had lived there,
a darkly warm feeling of being in a haven known
only to a few other people in the world. In more
practical terms, it was in fact the way in which
this minute stretch of softness, of feminine flank,

was caught between the great rough expanse of heather and rock and the measureless sea which gave Cragaig its particular qualities of unworldliness and peace.

Its name hinted at a history reaching back to the Norse settlements of Scotland but of the times beyond the hundred and fifty years prior to Alasdair's birth there were few facts readily available either in print or tradition. One of the peculiarities in the history of Cragaig was the way in which it had not been touched by the Clearances. All over the Highlands, and indeed the island itself, were ghostly monuments to these times, yet strangely Cragaig had escaped the flail. As a young boy Alasdair had heard his grandfather speak of these times, speak with thinly disguised fury and loathing of the happenings in villages only a few miles away. But Cragaig had just been that bit too remote, too poorly endowed with grazing land for the local laird to trouble himself. And so the village survived those smoking years and even by Alasdair's father's tenth birthday it was still a thriving community supporting some fifty souls.

But then several bad years had befallen them just at the time when news was infiltrating from the mainland that there was work to be had in the factories to the south. Nobody knew too much about the work involved but it was said to provide a steady wage, which in itself was temptation enough when the alternative was to watch

one's wife and children slowly flagging through
sheer malnutrition and cold. For those years had
been bad, as bad as any man would want to live
through, said Alasdair's father, and after the
third ferocious winter most of the families simply
gathered themselves together and left, their
loyalty to the village quite suddenly cracking
under the accumulated pressures. It was no
longer a question of trading in the simple wonders
of this life in a small ocean community for the
drabness of an industrial town and a little money;
it was the spiking, desperate call of an animal
instinct which drove them towards anything
which might provide a means of survival. And,
of course, once the move was made very few of
them ever came back to the island, let alone the
village.

But it so happened that Alasdair's aunt—his
father's sister—a young woman in her early
twenties but never of very strong health, had
suffered badly through these years so that when
the exodus began she was too weak to be moved.
And so it was that in the space of two months
more than forty people left Cragaig and only two
families remained—that consisting of Alasdair's
father, his sickly sister and their parents; and that
of two other older people with a spirited daughter
of thirteen with pitch-black hair and laughing
eyes. Within the year these seven people were
reduced to six for Alasdair's aunt who had been
the sole reason for their remaining at Cragaig,

ironically collapsed and died, just when everyone believed her to be strong again.

For six further years the little gathering flourished and it was only natural that Alasdair's father should have become close friends with the only other child of his age left in the village—the black-haired girl with laughing eyes. Then his mother—Alasdair's paternal grandmother—died and temporarily a cloud fell over their lives. Two years later the black-haired girl's parents were both taken poorly and it was decided that they should spend their last years in comparative comfort with some well-to-do relatives on the mainland. By this time it was an accepted fact that the girl would eventually marry Alasdair's father and since he was now twenty-three and she was twenty-one and since her parents were about to leave, the young couple were speedily proclaimed and were married within the month.

The girl's parents left and Alasdair's father joined his new wife in the house where until recently he had been paying strangely formal visits of courtship. Life and time moved on and in the second year of their marriage Alasdair was born to them. He was a docile child, apparently given to day-dreaming, but for two and a half years he was all his parents could want. Then his mother became pregnant again and it seemed as though their happiness were going to be crowned by a further joy. And so it was, for a second son was born to them, fair-haired, blue-eyed David, but his mother did not live to see him. There were complications at the birth and after an extended and exhausting labour she suddenly gave three short moans, followed by a blood-curdling scream and was dead.

Alasdair's father never quite recovered. During the first months after his wife's death he was pre-occupied by finding wee David a wet-nurse, feeding Alasdair and generally acting as both mother and father to the children. But as the children grew and slowly became more independ-ent their father lapsed into a melancholy which, over the years, came to rule his life.

Then one late summer's day when Alasdair was eight, his father and grandfather went out after a stag. It was long past dark when his father eventually returned, with the corpse of the older man over his shoulder. They had brought down a large stag on the other side of the hill and, dropping the gun, had hurried forward to bleed it. But the beast, though badly wounded was far from dead and when Alasdair's grandfather, forgetting himself in the heat of the moment, foolishly approached the stag from the front, up came the head and antlers as the animal rose to its feet, killing the old man outright. The blow not only broke his neck but opened up a horrible wound across the wattled old throat so that by the time Alasdair's father arrived home with his grisly burden he was nothing but a mass of blood and gore. Wee David, aged five, had screamed hysterically for an hour or more but Alasdair, in spite of vomiting twice, had quickly become calm of necessity and had busied himself placating his brother and doing his best to help his father clear up the mess. He did well enough but he was only eight and the scene impressed itself deep in the soft wax of his turbid mind. And so it came to be that there were just the three people left in Cragaig—the father and his two sons.

And with the depopulation so the material side of the village declined. Alasdair was born in the midst of a scene of decay and collapse. Of the original twelve houses only two were still inhabited at that date and the others stood miserably on the hillside, their slow death only occasionally hastened by the odd gale or the removal of a length of timber needed elsewhere.

The village had originally consisted of these twelve houses, neat dry-stone buildings set haphazardly within the confines of a low wall. They were of single-storey construction with the rounded corners peculiar to the Highland croft. The walls were of bare, grey stone, dug and quarried from the nearby hills and then split and shaped into rough rectangular blocks. Only the front of each building was relieved of monotony by a low doorway and two small windows. In earlier days their heaviness had been alleviated by roofs of rush and reed thatch but later with the scarcity of these materials and the lack of thatchers the old style was abandoned and replaced by more driftwood laths and sheets of poor corrugated iron.

Besides the houses the village also contained a large walled garden, the age-old kale-yard, where turnips and kale and potatoes grew easily enough in a soil which was rich after centuries of working. In the far corner of the garden, right under the shelter of the protecting hillock, an ancient ash tree grew. Below the garden, at the foot of the village, sang the burn, curving and meandering gently until it met the hillock where it turned again and disappeared down into the cavernous gullet and then tumbled and leapt into the air towards the sea.

After his father's death and his brother's departure, Alasdair Mór had stayed on in the family house and had simply maintained what remained of his mother's house for it to serve as a shed, a store-room and a byre for the animals. Around him stood the other houses, still recognisably houses but roofless and with one wall a flat bannock of rocks spreading on to the ground amidst clumps of nettles; the village wall, still a strong clear line but pitted with sudden holes, a gap-toothed blasted defence line; smaller piles of rubble half seen under the thick grass suggesting sketches of smaller buildings, mere cots. All around this small clifftop habitation, the wild land was working, working day and night over the centuries, silently, imperceptibly, to reclaim what it knew to be its own. A stone falling from above

29

the lintel of one of the ruins was a rare, enormous event but it was not such overt occurrences which marked the withering of this human foothold: it was rather the few extra blades of grass which sprang up unbidden and unnoticed each year, the motionless progress of the brackens and heathers down from the hills, ranging their ranks in profusion for the slow-motion breaching of the village wall in the nearest future.

And yet to Alasdair Mór as he rolled slowly home along the cliffs that warm evening there came no such dramatic and ominous thoughts. If Cragaig seemed less alive than it had thirty years ago, och well that was just the way things went. It must, in fact, be what Aulay so often spoke of as progress.

He came creeping up the last slope, his arms dangling low before him like superfluous limbs, occasionally snatching up pieces of heather which he examined minutely for a few seconds before casting them aside violently as if in a sudden fit of irritation. He came out on top and stopped. There he stood, shin-deep in the growth of the land, a black plywood shape against the roaring light of the sun. His right hand scratched violently at his thigh and then hung loose again and still he stood there.

How many times had Alasdair Mór thus come upon his village? Was there a past and future in his life or was his repetitive existence a long extension of the present? Having no sense of analysis, Alasdair was pure sensation. For what did it count if he had stood before this age-old scene on previous occasions? The effect was still as strong as ever and his blood warmed with pride. There he was with the warmth on his back reminding him of the flame-scattered sea and sky behind him and out in front, the hills climbing tawny and rust in endless layers towards the watered sky while in the hollow below, where the shadows lay among streaks of light, was his house.

His eyes, narrow again in his thinking face, ran over the building seeking out the details which were as landmarks in his life. The far end of the roof which he had stripped and recovered some summers back; the hole beneath the near corner where he had once found a large buck-rabbit sheltering; the patches of grass growing from between a crevice along the back of the building. . . . All these spoke of the long years, of security, of peace. He saw also the other building by which some of his hens were now pecking and saw in his mind the inside with its rank smells and black and white mosaics of hen-droppings and in a muddled flurry of half-formed memories there came to him pictures of his earliest childhood and the dim, but unmuffled scream that he had heard from his grandfather's house as wee David sprang into the world. Those long years ago.

As always happened when the dull stirrings of loneliness rose in his mind, Alasdair turned to his animals. He broke into a clumsy trot of un-coordinated limbs down through the tangling heathers and came out on to the sward.

The grass received his weight with a buoyancy, a welcome even. This was his homefield, the Norsemen's *tún*, the land nearest his home where the turf was as holy and close to a man's heart as one of his children. Here he walked with a new spring to his steps so that his tripping, unbalanced gait was suddenly transformed into small bounds of joy.

Down the gentle slope of the village grass he came and as he appeared round the corner of his house his brood of hens, a dozen in number, raised their heads and ran, as a single body, to meet him. They knew well enough that it was feeding-time but they ran towards Alasdair with more than hunger. They poured in upon his feet, a breaker of brown feather and pink comb, swirling and eddying about him as he marched on towards the hen house. Then he stopped and sank to his haunches in their midst. The clucking and rushing slowed to a quieter pace as Alasdair held out a big brawny hand. Some pecked at it while others slid in beneath his hams and between his legs.

'Och well, ye're fine now that I'm come home, are ye no? But all the same, it'll be your food ye're after, of that I'm sure.' A gurgling laugh. 'Ach, your beak's a hell of a sharp there. Can ye no wait a while for your food. Hey, away with ye.'

And laughs again as one of the hens pushes and bucks beneath him.

He stands up suddenly and the hens scatter and flap and half fly with much squawking. He walks quickly towards the shed, a light in his eyes as he feels himself master with his faithful friends trooping behind him. The mash is soon made and cast among the jostling mass of feathers and for a while he is forgotten.

Between the shed and the village wall he finds his little flock of sheep—a tup, six yowes and a few lambs. They, less extrovert creatures than his madcap hens, simply look up and watch as he approaches them. He catches hold of one of his yearling lambs and fondles it, feeling over its hindquarters for the roll of fat that will indicate the state of the animal's growth. One of the yowes, the mother of this lamb, looks round at Alasdair.

'And how is it with you the day, old woman? Yon lamb of yours is for being a right bonny one—there's a good weight on her already for her eighteen months. Ye'll be showing her the good grasses no doubt.' And another great laugh of pleasure at this unlikely image.

Alasdair leaves the lamb and yowe to themselves and visits his tup, a patriarchal beast, heavy-headed with its thick screwing horns, neck fleece bulged with muscle, long pendulous bag bumping between the hind legs. Alasdair holds him tight by one of the massive horns, runs his other hand appraisingly over the neck and back and seeks downwards to the scrotum which he weighs softly in his open palm. The tup stands unmoving, only its sleepy eyes blinking round towards Alasdair's face.

'A fine master. The very weight in them will give yon yowes a few more to care for. There's no rig in ye, is there now? Och and ye ken it too. The yowes need ye and there's no other who'd be for taking your place. Well, away with ye the now and on with the eating for we'll be needing the fat on ye for the winter.'

And Alasdair is up and patting the other sheep in turn before heading down to the big pool in the burn where his Highland cow is standing knee-deep in the water in defence against the warble flies. There she stands, still in a trance from the day's warmth, her fringe of hair between the massive symmetrical horns, head raised in anticipation, tail lashing at the flies. With her, Alasdair has a closer understanding than with the other animals and though he pats and strokes her with immense affection he talks less to her. Rather, he mumbles and croons and hums and sings to her as she, unbidden, follows him from the burn up to the shed for her evening milking.

In the warm half-light, deep in the arena of those circling hills, Alasdair and the cow settle down to their ritual. The old wooden box is placed, the pail accurately positioned beneath the swollen udder and to the tune of Alasdair's incantatory half-song the rhythm of his fingers begins to ply the teats. The first jets of milk sting into the empty bucket with a metallic ring and onwards the arms move till the sounds of the squirting milk change from harsh to rich as the bottom of the bucket fills. Upwards and downwards the chant climbs and falls like the wind-blown hawk and the cow stands in a haze of sleep and pleasure at the man's love for her. Without breaking the rhythm his hands move from one teat to the next and now as the tune reaches its peak his eyes close, his neck arches backwards and his nostrils flare and he is over-come by the entwined pulsations of milking and music padded by the smells of the sweet juice and the cow. But slowly the moment begins to unwind and the pitch of the song drops. And then with a sudden lack of flourish the milk and the tune are at an end and there he is sitting on the green of Cragaig with a brimming bucket of milk, himself and his grateful cow. He pauses for a second then quickly pats the cow. Man and beast walk apart.

Alasdair leaves the bucket on the flagged ledge outside his house and goes clucking and calling to his hens again. A few minutes later the last hen is secured inside the shed for the night. He walks back to the house, sighs deeply, picks up the pail and opens the door. With its well-known creak the door peels back on a room of cool gloom. Little can be seen except in the area immediately beneath the two windows where the evening light shows, on the one hand, a few creels in need of repair, a shuttle and a ball of twine, an old knife and a large coil of rope while on the other, a lobster box full of tools.

He puts down the milk and pushes the door to. Then, in the darkness he wanders off, snuffling and hawking and the shape of his frame is quite suddenly lost to sight. A silence broken by his occasional murmuring and sounds of exploratory hands fiddling with something. Then the noise of a match being extracted from its box and a second later the sharp-edged rasp of it being struck. And out of the darkness in the far right-hand corner a dull glow which seems to do no more than to give Alasdair's black hulk a corona of yellow fire while new, vague shapes around him flitter and jump in the unsteady light. But then a paraffin lamp is lit and a mixture of butter-soft brightness and wavering shadow illuminates the whole house.

It is a single room, some ten paces by five in size, with a floor of roughly shaped flagstones. In between these stones there is often as much as a half-thumb's length of mud and earth. Nearer the walls these fat little openings have put forth grass and small weeds. The walls of the room differ in no way from the outside of the building—a maze of bare stones, set and balanced to perfection but with no attempt at extra insulation or the added light which a quick coat of whitewash would have brought.

Up above, where the weak waxen light scarcely reaches, appear the outlines of the roof timbers, venerable lengths of wood now seemingly impervious to all agents of rot by their thick coating of soot and grease. Upwards and upwards like a church vaulting the cavity of the roof stretches so that the lines of the sarking beneath the corrugated iron are only partially discernible. They are distant shapes at night, a mere constellation in the sky of the roof where the intricate cross-structures of the beams are prominent. From one of the central beams hangs a motley of nets and ropes.

The room itself is simply divided. The end wall by which Alasdair has lit the lamp contains a large open fireplace. This end of the building by dint of being warmest, contains the basic living quarters. Before the cold black fireplace a simple wooden chair with a straight back. In the corner, between the fire and the window, Alasdair's bed—four heavy stones supporting what had originally been a door of one of the now ruined houses, five planks nailed together. A primitive mattress consisting of two large sacks sewn together and stuffed with dried heathers lies, bump and bulk, on the bed while a couple of threadbare blankets are crumpled up against the wall.

On the other side of the fireplace are a narrow table and a couple of shelves carrying his cooking utensils. There are two sooty pots, a mug, a couple of tin plates, three forks, a knife, a spoon with a twisted handle, a bowl of congealed potato and turnip soup, a pair of mackerel saved from a fate in the bait barrel, some salt, sugar, tea, matches and an end of bread. Also on the shelves are the lamp, some ammunition, another ball of twine and a large fish knife. This latter has a solid wooden handle and a simple but powerful blade, a full hand's length long and three fingers wide, which sparkles bright in the lamplight more from constant use than any particular care which Alasdair takes of it.

Below the shelves stand two silvery buckets full of water. Peaty water from the burn. Cold, still, golden-brown water held in silver. The real *uisge beatha*, the water of life.

The other end of the building which still lies in comparative darkness acts as a storeroom. Part of this is taken up by a stack of peats, those which are ready for burning, while the main bulk of his supply for the winter lies drying out in the other house. Then there are some small canisters of paraffin, the blade of a scythe and a brand new snead, an old but good rifle with a walnut stock and some fishing lines.

Alasdair Mór peered out through the window. With the falling heat the sky had begun to cloud over blotting out the thin rind of the moon which had just started to show itself. Now only a lack of real darkness in the sky spoke of the day which had been. The upper branches of the ash tree with their offshoot twigs and leaves stood

out against the ghost of light in the sky, shifting
and returning in the evening breeze like many
lobster claws.

Alasdair was glad to be home. But had he
ventured forth again he would have seen the
smooth shape of the hills becoming a range of
forts on the skyline. He would have heard the burn
tumbling mysteriously, invisibly in the darker
levels of its bed; and out through the gullet where
it fell, the half light on the sea shimmering,
drifting as a formless mist removing all sense of
perspective, making the watcher strain his eyes
to be sure that a familiar rock was not a whale.
This glimmering, shifting hour of the day would
cloud a man's mind from the logic to which he was
accustomed to resort in the light of the sun.

And with the waning visibility, a new consciousness of sound and smell. The steady turning
of the burn permeated everything. The slightest
bluster of wind not only brought the sound of the
tide slapping on the rocks below but also the
keenest smell of salt and tangle, the fish and
crunched crab piled possessively at the webbed feet
of the invisible skart. And the smell of heather,
heated and pressed by the day's long sun. And
other smells. The warm and oily waters of the
pungent peat-moss, the acrid vapours of the
sheep's fleeces in which tangled brackens and
roots combined as in a witch's pot to make a nose
twitch and inhale with sensation and pleasure.
And even high above in the air, where smells

were tenuous and few, there were sounds of moving life—the swish of the owl's wing, the rasp of an unoiled hinge as the heron tunelessly called out on its way home, the trill-and-unwinding-motor cry of a bunch of oystercatchers running the coast. So that the sky and land seemed more alive than in the full daylight, here in this evening hour when most eyes were sightless.

And then, of a sudden, Cragaig was devoid of all its character. At some unchartable point, the twilight broke and full darkness came. The old village with its atmosphere of long-standing security, this haven on the wild coast, a warming cluster of buildings and animals—all this vanished, dissolved or merged into the surrounding scenery so that the houses and walls became as the rocks and outcrops of the hills and the sward and burn were suddenly like any other piece of smoothed grass with a stretch of running water. Even Alasdair's house with its glimmer of light ceased to be a house with life inside and became no more than a block on a hill with a pinprick of light in some way superimposed on it. The animals were gone as were the comforting signs of life like the spade casually left against a wall, the planted garden, the mound of newly dug earth—all these were quite suddenly, no more.

This, then, was the night.

And so each day, for all anyone might do to prevent it, the land in a close alliance with the treacherous, deceiving sun gained back from men the little they seemed to have claimed for themselves. For on those barren shores it was in the light and heat that human existence showed itself and at this hour these small fluttering pennants seemed near to being destroyed for ever. The years had whittled away at the village until only its strongest and most obstinate inhabitant was left. Alasdair Mór, great in love as he was great in strength, held on to this life with a steeled and unmoving passion.

At that moment he sat by the remains of a small peat fire which he had lit more to heat the remains of his soup than for any need of warmth. Drinking straight from the bowl, he had golloped down the soup with loud drainings and swallowings, afterwards scooping out the pieces of potato left behind with his first finger which he then sucked with all the glee of a child. Then he had picked up the end of bread, and had ripped at it with his teeth, holding it in between mouthfuls in both hands on his knees and gazing into the fire as he chewed. He had finished his meal by dipping a cup into the bowl of milk and, after extracting a hair or two from the surface and looking inquisitively at the creamy juice, throwing the whole cupful down his throat in a greedy draught. He had put the cup down sharply on the stone floor, as if suddenly bored with it now that the meal was over, had wiped his mouth on his sleeve, farted absent-mindedly and then fallen into a state of half-thinking, half-dozing.

THE DEAD OF WINTER

He sat hunched forward on the chair, squeezing his fist with his other hand, his face taut with thought, his upper teeth biting into his lower lip. The peats fizzed and smoked and glowed giving out rich earthy smells into the room.

It would not be easy to say what he was thinking for as the first waves of sleep ran over him, his mind became a tangled pottage of thoughts. Things to be done the morrow, things to ask Aulay, things to be remembered—all confused with sudden visions of the past and mad ideas in no way connected with his life. His head nodded once, twice.

Outside, the night. The dull sound of surf.

Only minutes later the light in the house went out and Alasdair gave himself up to the darkness. The last stronghold of Cragaig had taken to the hills.

3

IT WAS only a few days later that winter arrived.

Normally it came peacefully enough, in a slow process of shortening days and choking mists followed by a series of storms but this year it rampaged in, tossing its head and stamping the ground, threatening the West Coast with a season of harsh cold and wild weather. Earlier, the long summer days had merged into an autumnal warmth which had stretched almost uninterrupted deep into the last months of the year. But the winter, long accustomed to being a dominant force in this part of the land, would not stand this delay indefinitely and each day Alasdair Mór sniffed the wind and scanned the long open sky for signs of its coming.

That evening he had gone to bed early. Although there had been only a stiff breeze in a clear sky at sunset, Alasdair had seen in distant clouds signs of unrest, signs that the dark season was impatiently approaching. He thought for the safety of his creels but it was already getting late and he decided to risk his luck. He had kicked off his tackety boots, thrown his jerkin and cap on the chair and climbed on to the bed, instinctively wrapping himself tightly in the blankets as if to

defend himself. He twisted and turned in the
darkness, half waiting for sleep, half tracking the
movements of the weather outside and thinking of his creels. But in those early hours of the
night nothing had come and Alasdair, finally
caught in the meshes of sleep, lost the scent of his
worries and closed his eyes.

In the small hours, he awoke. The sound of the
door shifting slightly as a wind pushed and
tugged at it. He lay there, eyes still closed, and
heard the open-handed cuffs of the wind against
the walls, the old gaffer wheezing of the wind
around the roof, the ever running sound of the
wind as it came in off the sea, furrowed up the
gullets, ran between the houses and made off into
the hills. Then, in a brief, strange lull, the first
prickles of rain on the corrugated iron roof. It
quickly built to a steady running of six hundred
thousand feet and then burst into blows of faggot-
bundled shafts of water before the pressure of the
wind. Again and again the wind lifted and swept
in with the rain in its claws, creating patterns of
sound on the windows and roof as if it were the
very surf of the sea.

A whole armful of rain ran up against the
window above Alasdair's head and he blinked and
thought again of his creels and the night outside.
But now the sound of the rain was sinking beneath
the ever increasing strength of the wind which
grew from small cries and shouts to large-scale
volleys and charges. Maddened herds came in

across the sea and careered over the surface of the land, banging painlessly into cliffs and rocks and houses, ricocheting helter-skelter back into each other so that everything revolved in a turmoil of sound. The rain fell no less, but was driven powerlessly before the scurrying hordes so that each ox-shouldered blast on the iron roof was punctuated by bristlings of water.

The violence of the wind continued to grow. Alasdair Mór lay awake feeling a pride in his house as it stood before this buffeting. His hands came up and felt the flexing of his biceps as if he and his house were one, together, bracing themselves against the onslaught of the storm. He raised his left hand and placed it against the cold wall by his head. He stroked the wall. Patted it.

'Aye, it's blowing. But it'll no be long.'

And the roof shuddered, showing its strength, as a roller of wind and rain broke over its back and cascaded down its sides. The door rattled wildly. The windows were stung again and again as they stopped rain as hard as gravel. The chimney never ceased an endless, atonal dirge.

But for all that Alasdair rallied his house in this moment of strife the storm's strength had long passed fighting with mere houses. This was the winter's vanguard throwing its first forces into the colonies of the land. The land stonewalled, holding itself motionless, waiting for the elements to exhaust themselves. Houses were forgotten.

Men had best lie low and hope that their houses did so also.

Cragaig drew in its neck and hunched down in the hollow. The animals stood resignedly behind the shed, the sheep tightly clustered together, eyes as vacant as it if were a still warm afternoon. Alasdair Mór, now that the storm had settled to a steady pitch, was dropping off again.

For several hours that storm wound and somersaulted its way about the cliffs and hills, stamping, laughing and growling in the excitement of attack and the voiceless earth dozed onwards seeming to ignore the maraudings of its agile aggressor.

Alasdair, too, dozed and fell into periods of fitful sleep. His face twitched and wrinkled and every few minutes he turned over, humping himself round in the cocoon of his blankets. In and out of his mind crept the vision of his creels at the mercy of the sea. He saw lines breaking, creels dragging, all his equipment scattered and sunk and these visions continued to prey on his mind as he lay halfway between sleeping and waking so that by the time dawn came his face was drawn and haggard.

But in the last hour before dawn the storm began to die. Like an overspirited child it had run itself to a complete standstill. Quite suddenly, in the last reaches of the night the rain stopped and minutes later the wind as well appeared to turn itself away in exhaustion and defeat. In his half-sleep Alasdair heard this happen, heard the cave of silence open around him, felt the great depth of his roof expand above him and as the tamed survivors of the wind puffed and wallowed on the cliff edge, he dropped backwards into an immense gulf of oblivion.

And then, with the storm gone and the coast suddenly at rest, the darkness prepared for dawn. Slowly but surely the remains of the wind slipped round towards the north and then died. Somewhere on the cliff, a bird, half-dozing under a bush, suddenly woke up and looked around inquisitively as the temperature began to fall.

An hour or so after first light Alasdair began to be restless in his sleep. Across the cold grey room his shape could be seen huddled on the bed, his knees drawn up and his head pulled down in an instinctively foetal position against the cold. The ashes lay grey powder of death in a blackened, arid fireplace. The soup bowl, icy to the touch, was covered in a thick crust of remains. His jerkin and cap, so easily cast on to the chair in the anticipation of sleep the evening before, now spoke of the past, crumpled signs of a day that would never be again. The nets and ropes hung despondently from the rafters.

Silence. The light outside unnaturally grey and dim. The sound, only, of a man breathing.

Then, without warning, a groan. Silence again. The man moves in his sleep. The sound of him swallowing; grinding his teeth. Small grunts.

And then, like a startled deer, he springs forward, sits up, eyes wide open.

The enormous rusty buoy, drifting out to sea with a broken line, is not real.

The man sits, propped by his arms behind him, staring.

He peers through the window and sees no more than a few feet beyond the house. Braes and muscles of fog wad and pad the house. Alasdair turns away.

He got up with a spring, his face clouded and set. It was cold in the room. Bits of metal—the spoon, the small poker, the lamp—all were burning with the new cold. Through the warmth of his thick socks, Alasdair felt the chill of the great floor-stones creeping towards his flesh with the silent guile of a blue fox.

Using a few pieces of peat which had remained only half-burnt from the evening before, Alasdair produced a fire large enough to boil some water on. He went to his two pails of water (now scarcely glowing in the thin light) and plunged a mug into the freezing depths of one of them. Some water splashed up on his wrist which still had the soft, tender warmth of bed on it and he started at the way the drops seemed to cut through to his bones. But soon enough a little pot was balanced over the fire and there were hissings and poppings and vague signs of steam.

As he wandered round the room waiting for the water to boil Alasdair thought of little but his creels. He knew well that the storm had been bad enough to cause a lot of damage to them. And he knew that a large loss of tackle at this stage in the year would be disastrous for him. But then again these storms and squalls were strange, unpredictable things. For the state of the sea depended as much on the position of the tides and currents in relation to the wind as it did on the wind itself. And all this was sheer luck. So Alasdair Mór went on pacing the room impatiently, wanting his cup of tea but at the same time eager to get down to the shore and find out what had happened. And if he had to lose any creels he just hoped that it would be the ones by the rocks where the otters had been last year. Those creels were in very poor condition and would soon have to be thrown out. But he feared that his fortune might have it that the sea had taken the two sets of creels which were at the mouth of the burn. These were not actually new but he had almost completely rebuilt them about a month ago. He had made a special expedition some eight miles up the coast where, in a secluded corner, the hazel trees grew. He had spent most of the morning cutting lengths of the pliable wood–stopping every now and again to eat a handful of the nuts which ripened so well in that place where the sun and not the winds came–before walking home with an enormous bundle of sticks on his back. Then the pieces of wood had had to be bent and shaped and fastened to the base, after which the netting had to be attached and the two entrances contrived. And finally the whole creel had to be tarred. One month ago only.

He stamped around the stone-flagged floor, expelling violent signs of irritation, waiting on the little pot of water. But it only shivered and steamed and shivered again as if it could never boil. Alasdair roddled away at the peats and a second later up came a whole branch of lively flames. A minute later the water boiled and the tea was made. But the cup of tea was only half drunk when Alasdair put it down and made for the door.

He pulled it open and hurried outside. As the wood closed with a dull bang behind him Alasdair found himself deep in another world. At first he saw more or less nothing. He was caught in a crowd of opaque shapes taller than himself whose shoulders and torsos turned and rippled endlessly. Sometimes he caught the swirling action of one of these figures full in his face but felt nothing and came out on the other side into a new crowd.

The fog seemed literally trapped in the hollow. The stillness was a miracle—not a movement apart from the slow-motion convolutions of the fog which appeared to have an existence completely independent of the rest of the scene. And the few sounds which rose to Alasdair's ears were equally astonishing in their purity and isolation. There were the sounds of Alasdair himself crunching along over the crystalled grass—his feet, his heart, his pennant of breath. There was the tumble of the burn, strangely muffled yet quite clear. There was the steady, repeated bleat of a sheep somewhere to the left in the fog. And, as if in answer to this, there was the long deep boom of the fog-horn rolling down through the morning silence from the point many miles to the north. And covering and surrounding all these sensations was the cold, the sharp, damp cold of fog which creeps and crawls through many layers of clothing and leaves a man with frost in his gut.

But even as Alasdair walked through the village where odd walls loomed up like keeps of deserted castles, even as he wandered through this place which had little or no connection with Cragaig as he knew it, so the sun's bright rays started pricking and poking through cloud and fog, letting it be known that the wide heavens of sea and sky were not far away.

And so Alasdair pushed urgently onwards with the foghorn casting lugubrious, leaden weights about the insecurity of his hope. The heathers carried the frost as if it were a dusting of glittering flour; the water of the peat moss was frozen enough for there to be a slight cracking sound before Alasdair's boots sank into the muddy waters. The brackens had come to the end of their year: with this first freezing the tip of each fern would now start to take on the yellow, the brown of withering, of death.

And then as he strode through these frozen bristles and canopies, Alasdair broke out of the thicket of dense fog caught behind the escarpment and found about him the lemon-sharp colours of an early winter's day.

The fog at Cragaig was by no means the only fog on the coast. In fact, there was fog sprawling everywhere, over both sea and land but it was broken and patchy so that the view was like an incomplete jig-saw puzzle. There were sections of the sea which can rarely have appeared so primevally pure. For they lay like the blue-green backs of women, only the slightest undulations of spine and ribs and shoulder blades and, beneath, the intimation of infinity. On these plateaus the sun shone and then vanished and then shone again before the light was lost in the fogginess and clouds of the upper air so that the waters, in pursuit, flashed and lay dull and then rose again to life. And in this process the vapours floated opaque and glowing by turn as the wild-mad sun climbed ceaselessly into the sky.

Along the coast the land was laden and hung with clouds of fog. It lay, as at Cragaig, rolled and bundled in depressions and hollows on the cliffs; it hung like sheep's wool on barbed wire, caught on clusters of dwarf birch and deep brackens on the steep drop to the shore; it lay, strangely, on one tract of water and not on another; it masked cliffs and exposed hills; great fingers of it rudely explored cracks and creases of the coast, snaking silently in and then lying smugly satisfied. The animals came and went in this disturbed world. The Achateny sheep, far below by the shore, and Alasdair's own handful up by the village, wandered in and out of the fog, bleating at their misfortune as they cropped their way into a patch and were lost.

Alasdair laughed to himself. How those sheep contrived to find difficulties! And yet he was not laughing at them for they were only his fellow creatures and his friendship had no room for contempt. That the sheep were not so good at helping themselves was an irrevocable, painless fact and one which awoke feelings of sympathy in Alasdair. For Alasdair, too, was a sheep in the world.

But now he was hurrying on, quick stepping down the cliff path to Port nam Freumh through small, thick, fistfuls of fog, moving all the time with the surefootedness of a rabbit in a warren. Down a step and he would let the whole side of his body drop so that the rolling motion was accentuated. Occasionally there was a large fall in the path and here he would jump and land heavily on both feet, grunting aloud at the moment of impact.

There was no great beauty of movement in his descent but the urgency with which he came down the steep path was a thing to see. For Alasdair, with his mind set solely on the safety of his creels, came down that path faster than caution would have allowed in such conditions but his desire and conviction were so great that it was as if he were bulldozing both physical ineptitude and the danger before him so that he slid and leaped and turned as if invulnerable. Faster and faster he came, his small, slightly pigeon-toed steps never lengthening but always speeding on. The path vanished into the head of a fog patch and Alasdair, without hesitating, plunged in. A great scattering sound of stones. A sheep charges out of the fog in terror. A further scattering as Alasdair takes a hairpin and drops over a large rock. Then the capped figure reappears, arms flailing, shoulders rolling and with a thundering final descent he issues out on to the upper beach.

When he came down to Port nam Freumh he passed the boat and went out to the rock at the end of the jetty. From the top of this he surveyed the sea. Great grey-green leads of water between islands of fog. Sure enough several of his buoys could be seen and they appeared not to have dragged too much. This was reassuring but there were others to be checked and so he turned, sprang down from the rock and made for the boat.

He collected the oars from behind a rock, filled a box with bait and jumped into the boat. He pushed off and began to pull strongly out into the oiled sea. Soon he had rounded the rock and was heading north up the coast. He examined one buoy, two buoys and their creels and found that not only was the tackle not damaged but that the creels also held some lobsters. A smile appeared in his eyes.

He thrust his arm into a creel and quickly took

hold of a lobster, grasping it expertly across the back so as to keep clear of the vicious pincers. The clinker-built tail opened and shut furiously as the lobster sought to get purchase on something, while the feelers and pincers waved about pathetically. The mottled blue carapace was of ice-cold steel. But here Alasdair was at home. He had that lobster tight between his knees, gripping it lightly but firmly and before the struggling creature knew what was happening its pincers were secured with lengths of twine and it was discarded in a box in the stern of the boat.

Alasdair moved on up the coast. One moment he was neatly silhouetted against a serpent of fog and the next, with only a split second of fading in between, he had vanished. For quarter of an hour there was no sign of him. Just the stifled sound of oars and rowlocks and buoys and creels. Splashings, squeaks, bangings and scrapings. And when eventually he did come forth from exactly the same valley in the stationary fog cloud as he had gone into, he was grim faced. Deep in that fog he had found a creel missing—the last on a set of three which had most probably dragged and caught against a rock thereby breaking the line. And although he had now checked more than half his creels and had only found one missing, a mood of senseless pessimism made him fear for the rest rather than rejoice in his luck so far. The others, his precious creels to the south of Port nam Freumh. . . .

THE DEAD OF WINTER

And so now Alasdair Mór's boat was to be seen working its way southwards, past Port nam Freumh to the mouth of the Cragaig burn and beyond. Alasdair rowed at a heavier, fixed pace without his initial energy as if he were unwilling to get to the other creels. Still the fog lay on the water and the boat slipped in and out of the patches like a beast passing through the undergrowth. The light was for ever shifting, the higher zones of fog and the clouds at one minute blotting out everything so that the sea was flat and sullen, the next opening themselves for the squirting shafts of sunlight to shower their strength on a sea of mysterious, diaphanous tissues. And so too the boat was changing. Now it was a heavy thing stalking across an arid sea then—o what joy!—it was an elegant line of power and movement riding fast and only skin-deep on a field of flashing fire.

At last Alasdair Mór reached the buoys to the south. Intact. And so not only were his prize creels at the burn unscathed but he had also a good catch of lobsters with the loss of only a single creel. What strange luck! And he rowed back with a delighted half-smile on his face and a full box of lobsters at his feet.

Today, life was good. Like all good luck it brought the excitement of surprise. For the storm had been bad enough to have ripped up and scattered his tackle over the depths. . . . He wondered how An Sionnach had fared. From the

way he had felt the wind in the night and from
the way his creels had survived he imagined that
An Sionnach's part of the coast must have borne
the brunt of the storm.

'Och, but yon's a hell of a canny. He'll have
had his creels in the while.'

Alasdair spoke aloud to himself, suddenly feeling the need to break the grim silence of anxiety
which had hung over him in the last hour. He
spoke of An Sionnach as if he knew him, in actual
fact basing his judgement purely on what he had
heard from Aulay and the others. But he was also
swayed by an instinct of respect, the respect of
incomprehension and awe for an unknown quantity, to which there was added, paradoxically, a
degree of contempt. And this odd mixture of
feelings came from the fact that An Sionnach
was a foreigner—a Scot and an islander, but a
man from out there, be it the Long Island or the
Orkneys. And Alasdair had known from an early
age that such foreigners were to be treated not
simply as different but as people with whom you
could never be sure of yourself. Though this
unthinking scorn, or mistrust, for foreigners was
strangely tempered by feelings of awe. Foreigners,
for all their suspicious difference, knew of things
which Alasdair could never know; had, perhaps,
special crafts and ways which helped them. And
An Sionnach, according to Aulay and the men on
the boats, had other things about him too; things
which men hated talking about but which they

all sensed. Alasdair had never seen this hidden neighbour but the talk of the men who had, opened Alasdair's imagination to the edge of fear, or rather a desire simply to avoid this man, for fear was something which rarely touched Alasdair's life. It would be better to keep a civil tongue towards An Sionnach, both to his face and behind his back.

By now the moving sun had soaked up most of the fog and the few large clouds of it which remained all lay upon the sea. Alasdair turned and looked up at the cliffs of Cragaig as he rowed. He saw the blue sky and remembered that there had been a blue sky the day before as well. But what a difference! For now the freezing air had sucked the essence of the colour from the sky, leaving it refined, delicate, the glow of blue seen through semi-transparent layers of ice. The cliffs and hills stood clear in the sun but everything glistened and shivered and was white with frost. The colours of the land looked as if milk had been stirred into them. Bushes and small trees, packages of frozen movement, stood like explosions on the slopes; rocks lay under great flashing nets of ice where water from the hillside normally trickled over them; and parishes of frozen brackens, often taller than a man, seemed like wonderful polar forests. From behind the cliff Alasdair's cow mooed long and clear. The air of the new season was biting amorously into the land.

Alasdair came back to himself. He had been

thinking of the winter and considering how much hay he could afford to get from Achateny for the animals. He had been wondering if the winter were going to be as hard as men were saying. And he was surveying that coast of his, seeing both the glory of the flowering cold and, in the same things, the threats to himself and his animals over the coming months. All the while he pulled thought-lessly at the oars, no longer bending his back into a sweeping stroke but just dipping the blades and giving one sharp clip of a tug on them. Behind him, one of the last patches of fog squatted lazily beneath the cliff.

Alasdair came back to himself and remembered that the collection boat would soon be round on one of its last calls. Not only did he have the box of lobsters in the boat but also several others which were waiting in the water at Port nam Freumh. He returned to his more urgent rhythm of rowing and the boat sprang forward and disappeared into the fog.

He headed for Port nam Freumh guided more by his instincts than by anything he could actually see. The fog clung to him, settled in his clothes, caught in the stubble on his face, choked him as he breathed, twisted all perspectives in his vision, seemed to catch on the blades of the oars between strokes and he longed to be free. But the harbour lay within.

He arrived back at Port nam Freumh and was in the middle of doing up the last box when he paused. He remained bent double, with his hands on a lobster and his head cocked sideways towards the sea. Had he heard a shout? Only the silence and the drifting fog and the slipping of the sea's edge rang in his ears. He turned back to the lobsters.

'Alasdair! are ye there?' The shout came sidling through the fog and found Alasdair swathed in smoking chains on the jetty.

'Aye I am that. Stay where ye are and I'll be out to you.' Alasdair's reply was a big-bellied roar with the sharp edge on it that came from little practice in shouting.

He loaded the boxes into the boat and leapt in after them. He was overeager and almost capsized the boat but managed to keep his balance and was straightaway poling off from the jetty with one of the oars. He rowed powerfully, pausing every few strokes in an attempt to pick up the distant puttering of the collection boat's engine.

The collection boat, a converted fishing vessel with a large hold, lay blue and orange a few yards off the outer edge of the bank of fog. One man leaned against the doorway of the wheelhouse while his younger brother paced the deck.

'Come on, you bastard, it's too raw the day for waiting on ye like this.' The older man mumbled further abuse more to express the chill in the air and thereby to will it away from himself than for any dislike of Alasdair. His brother went on pacing the deck, occasionally kicking at a hank of rope, occasionally glancing up at the fog.

'Where's yon bugger got to now?'

And at that a half shape loomed up in the fog and the black, swan's-neck curve of a boat's bows slipped forward out of the clouding vapours and was soon followed by the cap-and-jerkin rear view of Alasdair Mór.

'Raw enough the day.' Alasdair pauses. 'How are ye keeping then?'

'Och, well enough but I could do without yon bastarding fog. We'd a hell of a time coming round Caliach in it especially with the tides being as they are the day. And how are ye yourself? Did ye miss any creels in the night? It'll no have been that quiet round here I'm thinking.'

'Aye, it was kind of wild right enough.'

Alasdair is meanwhile standing up in the boat handing the boxes of lobsters to the younger brother who, without ever speaking, puts them down in the hold.

'It seems they had a bad time of it out Ardnamurchan way too. Willie MacFarlane and the boys were near on two hours late coming over this morning. They'd taken a hell of a battering in the night. And I'll believe it'll have been even worse up Mallaig way. They'll have had a bad time altogether.'

'Aye, they'll have had a bad time altogether.'

'Is that the last one, Alasdair?' Now it is the younger man who speaks.

'Aye, it is that.'

'Right then. Five boxes. Here ye are.' And he counts out some coins and hands them to Alasdair who immediately slips them into his trouser pocket and stands with one hand over the bulge they make. 'We'd best be away or Angus will be wondering where we've got to. You'll have heard about An Sionnach I'm thinking?'

'No. And what was that?'

'Well yon bugger certainly took the bad luck. He's missing all but two creels after yon storm and it's no as if those he missed were old ones. It'll have no been more than the month ago that he bought them. We called in as usual to take his boxes and there he was, the man himself, out in his boat by Stac an Aoineidh. I asked him how many boxes he had for us and, by Christ, as long as I live I'll mind the face of yon bugger when he looked at me. It was not so much what he said for the man's a hell of a close with words but the eyes in him were worse. They near as cut my tongue from my mouth. It turned out that he was not out to meet us but to try and find some of his tackle. Well, he'd got the two creels and that was the lot. A bad business.'

'A bad business right enough.' Alasdair's eyes sank thoughtfully to the bottom of his boat.

'Well, as I say, we'd best be away. Cheerio the now, Alasdair. We'll see you here the once more, on Tuesday.'

'Cheerio boys.'

And the larger boat with an open-throated coughing was moving off in a crescent that would take it round the fog and away to the north.

Alasdair Mór sat and let the wash of the vanishing boat rock and sway him as he thought over the news. Nobody had had a good word for An Sionnach from the day he arrived . . . but Alasdair knew what losing one's tackle could mean to a man who was just scraping a living from fishing and he was sorry for him. He wondered how An Sionnach would manage. Though there were always these tales of him having a bit of money. But of course there were two of them to provide for.

And he turned to see the patch of fog thinning, dissipating under the growing warmth of the morning sun. What had been an impenetrable solid was gradually starting to move, to twist and, in the coils of its twisting, to shrink. By the time he had rowed through it back to the coast, the patch had virtually gone and the full light of the sun was shining down on the measureless widths of the sea.

Alasdair, squinting ferociously, looked up at the sun. The new sun, the winter sun. A chill lemon of fire this morning, a blood orange this evening. The new season was here and all was well with Alasdair.

A skart winged its way northwards, its flight low and desperate. A heaviness settled on Alasdair's mind.

4

'HELLO there, Alasdair!'

'Hello. Cold enough the day.'

'Aye, it's sharp. And it'll no be getting warmer, right enough.'

Three days had passed since the storm. Three days of calm weather with a sharpness in the air which, after the autumn days, seemed like the steel jaws of a trap. Each morning Alasdair had scraped away the thin coating of ice from the inside of the window with his fingernails and peered out on a scene of frost and silence. He had squeezed the pads of his fingers so that the ice from the window had oozed out from under his nails and then he had stumped around the room while the fire had got under way. When at last the water had boiled and he had made his tea he drank it greedily, still marching around. A great draught of scalding liquid and the painful pleasure of it burning down his throat and into his stomach had made Alasdair gasp and wince, his face contorted, his teeth gritted. Then he would sit down by the fireplace, leaning forward with his elbows on his knees, and stare into the flickering, crackling peats. Perhaps he was still only half awake. He was in a stupor. The mug rested in his hands, tilted so that tea spilt out on to his boots from time to time but he was unconcerned, his eyes fixed on the hearth, his mind far away.

Outside, the early morning was pinned by the frost. It froze heavily during these nights. In the last hours of darkness the countryside was covered with a thousand kinds of crackings and snappings as plants became brittle under the cloak of cold. The sheep wondered if they were on some bed of pebbles when they moved and heard the crunchings beneath their hoofs and when they nibbled at the crisp grass their throats were filled with a rough chill. Up on the hillside the blackcock wriggled themselves deeper into the heathers. The whinchats, the stonechats, the hawk, the hoodie and the buzzard all drew in their necks, sinking their heads into their breast-feathers as did the oystercatchers, the gulls, the skarts and the other birds of the shore. Even the pair of eagles high on the rocks above the village blinked and shifted as the cold spread across the land.

At last, far out behind the hills, the sky became less black and then grey and finally the skyline itself started to leak out thin threads of whiter light. Even in this weak light the headland showed itself to be gripped by a tight web of frost whose white meshes fitted themselves to the contours like a trawl-net round a haul of cod. A light wind scarcely moved the stiffened brackens. The sea appeared frozen solid in its expanses of clouded waters.

THE DEAD OF WINTER

The full daylight came slowly and if the air seemed to grow warmer it was the illusion brought by the white sun above. As always, Alasdair went to sea but he rowed with a mad vigour, trying to keep some semblance of warmth in his bones. While he rowed he grimaced and twisted his face, the movement in the skin enough to maintain the flow of blood. But once he was out on the creels it was hopeless. The first contact with the water and the hauling of the long, soaking line were initially stimulation to his hands but slowly the damp and cold began to crawl like worms into his flesh. Then a small wave would break against the boat and the spray would cover him with burning barbs of fire. And after his hands had smouldered with cold for a while then, gradually, numbness set in so that by the time he was on to the second or third set of creels he hardly noticed when an agile lobster managed to nip his fingers. When he had lifted and reset all his creels his face and hands were bloodless, drops of water running over deathlike, waxen skin while his lips were pressed together in a mauve line as he struggled home. Once back at the house he would fumble with the matches, taking a full half-minute to extract one from the box with his useless hands. Eventually, when the fire was relit and the tea once more made he would go through the same process of revival as before.

Now, early in the afternoon, he had walked

the mile and a half along the cart-track from
Cragaig to the road. Aulay often passed the
road-end on his way from Achateny to the shops
and twice a week he waited for a few minutes in
case Alasdair should appear.

Alasdair had come down off the boggy plateau
which lay up on the hills behind Cragaig to see
Aulay's hunched figure sitting on the cart by the
roadside. As he came lumbering down the slope
Aulay's two dogs came barking and racing, bellies
close to the ground. A few seconds later they were
jumping up at Alasdair, circling him, getting
under his feet in a mad display of recognition.
Alasdair laughed and pushed the dogs down,
appearing to take little notice of them as he
walked on. And the black and white dogs jumped
and barked the more, egged on by Alasdair's
apparent refusal to play with them. And so the
trio poured off the hill, the man holding a straight
course downhill while the animals revolved
around him in every possible combination of two
ellipses about a moving point. Up above, the sky
was clear and a sparrow hawk hovered in a silent
trill.

By now Alasdair could see Aulay clearly. He
was an older man than Alasdair, somewhere in
his mid-sixties, thin with rounded shoulders and
a skin weathered like a walnut. Deep blue eyes
looked out from under short but prominent eyebrows. He sat, watching, on the bench seat of the
cart, his knotted spatulate hands clasping a

shepherd's crook. In the shafts of the small cart, a garron stood patiently, its head drooping like a heavy bag.

Aulay had been at Achateny since his late teens. He remembered Alasdair's birth. Later, he had been one of the few people who had come out to Cragaig to help with the animals when Alasdair's father was bed-ridden and the boys were out with the boat. Since wee David left those many years back he had been Alasdair's only constant link with the world. And yet for all the years that they had known each other one would have thought they were meeting for the first time, casual strangers on a road. For the warmth that these Highland folk felt for each other was something invisible, something rarely expressed. Help and be helped was the way of affection among them. Aulay watched Alasdair approaching as he had watched him approach twice a week year after year.

'Hello there, Alasdair!'

'Hello. Cold enough the day.'

'Aye, it's sharp. And it'll no be getting warmer, right enough.'

A pause. Alasdair pats one of the dogs. The dog turns and licks his hand.

'I was thinking that I must be getting in some hay for the winter. Will ye be keeping me some as usual?'

'Aye, I will that. When'll ye be wanting it?'

'Och, in a week or two.'

'Right.'

'Here, did ye ken that Douglas is marrying on to Janet Farquharson before the end of the year?'

'Janet Farquharson? Will she be to do with Farquharson of Penalbanach?'

'Och no. Oh . . . but ye'll no ken her for she's no that long over here. Her folk are from Seil. She came last Easter to work in the hotel and was stopping with her cousin Alec George. And Alec's a good friend of Douglas. Well, Douglas has got himself a good job now with the boats and a house to himself after his father's death so it was right he should get himself a woman. Och, and a bonny lass too. Are ye no thinking of getting married yourself?' A wild sparkle in Aulay's old blue eyes. Alasdair shifts from foot to foot and his eyes quickly move away from Aulay and come to rest on the distant hillside.

'No. . . . There'll be time enough yet.'

'Aye. Right enough.' And a silence ensues in which neither man is embarrassed but both are searching for something to say to fill in a gap. Aulay, who married at the age of fifty-one, is for ever twitting Alasdair about his single state. With no malice, for he really believes that Alasdair may still marry.

'And how's Martha keeping?' Martha, Aulay's wife, a year or two older than him. A short, rabbit-faced woman who bakes good bread and often sends some over to Alasdair.

'Och, she's well enough the now. Though she

was gey poorly last week. She took a terrible go of the 'flu and I thought she'd never be up from her bed again.'

'Martha's a hell of a hardy,' said Alasdair as if talking to himself.

'Aye, she is that.'

'Come here!' Aulay's sudden ferocious shout as one of his dogs starts to worry the Achateny cattle way over on the hillside. The dog halts immediately, looks round and then streaks back through the heathers to arrive panting and joyful by the cart. It was as if the shout had been a reward.

'And how's yon cow of yours with the whoor of a wound on her?' asks Alasdair.

'Ach, no so good. McLaren is after coming to see her and says it's the cancer.'

'No!'

'Aye. It's the cancer right enough and the sooner we could slaughter her the better for her. But she's still the calf with her so we'll have to be waiting a while yet. . . . I was over with Johnnie for the sales at the end of the week. It was the yowes on Wednesday and the stirks on Friday. I did hell of a poor with the stirks. Hell of a poor altogether. Ye should have seen yon beasts on the mainland. Yon stirks were more like my cows in size. A whoor of a size altogether. But I'd a better time with the yowes. We were over with forty blackface and thirty crosses and we'd a good price for them. And we'd finished by two o'clock,

so Johnnie and I were away to the hotel for a
shandy. By Christ, by the time we came to take
the last boat back Johnnie was hell of a full.
And I'd a good shot on me, too.' Here Aulay's
eyes are alight again at the very memory of the
alcoholic fires. Alasdair's face, too, creases and
splits into quiet laughter at this most Highland of
understood innuendoes—the image of liberation
through alcohol. But Aulay is rising to the
occasion and wants to complete the story of his
escapade.

'We had a few on the boat and were planning
on getting home with Adam and Calum the
Graves but then we stopped off for a half in the
village and by the time we'd finished the boys
were away so we had to walk home.'

'Did ye get a rowing from Martha?'

'Aye, well . . . aye, I did so.' And Aulay smirks
ruefully.

Quite suddenly a wind gets up, springs up from
behind the line of hills beyond the road, winnows
through the little group and vanishes again,
leaving nothing but the soft rocking of a breeze
behind it. It is enough to stop the conversation in
its tracks for a few seconds. The eyes of both of
them narrow as the cold air strikes them but then
Aulay is off on another tack.

'How were ye in the storm? I was thinking that
a southwesterly like that would be hitting ye bad.'

'Aye, well it was blowing right enough. And it
was damp.'

'But ye didne lose your creels, I hear.'

'Och no. Just the one. But I was hell of a lucky. A wind like that could have taken them all.'

Silence. Aulay pokes at the ground with his crook. The garron shifts impatiently. Aulay looks at the garron, at Alasdair and then back at the ground and continues to poke at the grass. Alasdair is cutting his nails with a large-bladed penknife.

'Did ye hear about An Sionnach?' Aulay ventures this one slowly.

'Aye I did that. From the boys on the boat the morning after the storm. It was hard on the bugger.'

'Aye it was that. I was in the village last night having a few halves. Angus and Calum the Graves and Adam were in too. We were having a grand time. We'd been there since six-thirty and we will have had quite a few. Oooh . . . and Bobby Felmer was there and he was a hell of a drunk. Sitting on the floor singing his head off. . . . What was I saying . . .? Oh yes . . . well, it was after leaving half past eight when the door opened and in came An Sionnach. Och, he was no looking a hell of a happy and, by Christ, ye should have heard the way everyone stopped talking when they saw him. True enough, they started again but it's bad the way yon bugger has the power on people. Aye, yon's a bad bugger. Well, as I was saying, An Sionnach comes in. He's already a skinful on him, but he comes up to the bar and

buys a half-bottle and a gill. Normally, I'd no go
out of my way to talk to the man, but it suddenly
came to me to say something. Perhaps it was the
drink . . . I couldne say. Well, I turned to him and
asked him if he'd managed to recover any of his
creels. "And what's that to you?" the man
replied, turning and staring at me with yon
terrible eyes of his. "And what's that to you?" he
repeated with a hiss in his voice and his eyes
narrowed like a snake. "Well," I said to him "I
was after wondering if ye'd managed to find any
of the tackle ye'd lost. I'd heard right enough that
ye'd been a hell of an unlucky with the storm and
was thinking to myself that ye might have
recovered a few creels." "Well I didne do so."
And with that the man turned away and stood
leaning on the bar. Well, I saw that with him
being so sour I'd best get back to the boys. So we
had another round or so and I suppose we'll
have been drinking another twenty minutes
when I happened to glance round and see that
An Sionnach was still standing there. The bugger
didne seem to have moved. There he stood with
his elbows on the bar and his eyes fixed in front
of himself and oh! by Christ, one hell of a look on
the man's face. He seemed to be deep in thought
for every now and then yon forehead of his would
knit something terrible. Well I canne mind how it
happened, but I suppose I will have been looking at
him for suddenly the man's around on me and
asks me what I'm after. "Och, nothing," I say, "I

was just looking for George MacFarlane" which the man must have known was no true for he comes up close to me, so close that I'm feeling his breath on my face. "Ye're all the same," he says with a bad bite to his voice. "Ye're all the same. Ye canne let a man in peace. What's it to you that I lost my creels. Can I no have my life to myself. I'm thinking ye'll just be watching me and asking me questions so that you can tell yon pleased bastard at Cragaig about it. The bugger sits there all pleased with himself and you buggers are away to tell him how I lost all my creels when he lost none. I'll tell ye what it was that saved his creels—luck, pure bloody luck. And he'll be there thinking how clever he's been and laughing at me. Well, by Christ, I'm telling ye yon bugger had best watch himself for one of these days I'll be showing him." And with that he turned on his heels and was way out of the bar. Och, I'm telling ye, the way yon man spoke to me was enough to put the fear of God into one. Yon's a whoor of a man altogether.'

'Aye, he'll be a queer one right enough.' Alasdair had listened to this story without opening his mouth, occasionally looking up from cutting his nails, occasionally scratching his ear. Now he stood there looking down at the sculpted nails of his left hand and wondering about An Sionnach.

Aulay, too, had wondered about An Sionnach the night before on the way home from the hotel. He had understood the man's bad humour, for the loss of the creels was a serious blow; but he could not forget the vicious fury with which he had spoken of Alasdair. And he had never even met Alasdair. It hardly seemed right. But it seemed to Aulay that An Sionnach was not a man who could be judged by ordinary standards. After all, he was from up north.

'Yon man, An Sionnach, is a queer one. He was none too polite when I asked him about the creels the night. I'm thinking that we should be keeping an eye on him.' This is what Aulay had said to Martha as they lay side by side in bed in the dark that same night; and Martha, tired out by a long day, had said 'Aye, it seems so' and had fallen asleep.

Now Aulay sat on the bench seat clasping his crook and watching Alasdair, who seemed deep in thought as he pared the nails of his other hand. The two dogs sat between Alasdair and Aulay, their pink tongues lolling, their flanks heaving. The garron shuddered. The cloud-flecked sky stretched taut above their heads.

But there was nothing more that could be said about An Sionnach's strange behaviour. So Aulay asked Alasdair what he needed from the town and Alasdair gave him a small list of things, mainly supplies of food.

And so, with a few more minutes of conversation in which the summer was reviewed and the coming winter foretold, the meeting was at an end. With a shake of the reins and a word

of farewell to Alasdair, Aulay began to move
away with the garron's croup rising heavily up
and down and the two dogs, noses to the ground,
following out scents and trails around the course
of the cart while all that became of Aulay himself was a pair of hunched shoulders with a small
head sunk into them.

Alasdair stood where he was until the cart had
creaked and groaned its way up the slope and
disappeared over the top. He plucked a small
branch of heather from the ground and stood
there twisting its root backwards and forwards
until his hands were covered with mud and
juices. Then, for no apparent reason, he dropped
it and his arms hung uselessly at his sides. His
face was gloomy, full of an uncharacteristic
despair as if the mind contained within the great
frame had suddenly found itself to be vulnerable.
Was this, in fact, what had happened? Perhaps;
but the mind of Alasdair Mór was dense and
complex and few things ever took on great
clarity in it. For sure, the instincts of survival
pulsed strong enough through his life and it could
have been that this latest news of An Sionnach had
touched upon and awoken one of these. Why
should a stranger take a dislike to him and his
way of life without ever having met him and
when the man had only been on the island a
matter of months? He, Alasdair Mór, who had
lived at Cragaig for forty-five years without
anyone so much as bothering about him. True, he

had hit a man once, but that was, wait . . . not far
off twenty-three years ago now. The man had
been drunk and had gone for Alasdair one
summer's day on the road to the town. Alasdair
had humoured the man for a while and then, in
exasperation, planted his fist on the side of the
man's head so hard that he had never known
what had hit him. And that was the only moment
of open hostility that he had ever had with anyone
in all those years. So why now was this An
Sionnach building up such hatred for him?

Alasdair felt the blood of defensive anger
worrying through his head. He saw again Ina and
Jennie and Wee Jamie laughing at him at school
hounding him mercilessly and he wanted to run
back to Cragaig as he had run home from school.
He turned and started to stumble up over the
tussocks and heathers, groaning and grunting to
himself in subdued anger. He fell once but
scrambled to his feet again and ran on, his great
bulk rolling more than ever. Up a steep slope he
stormed and slipped and slithered and ran on
again. On and on he forged, tripping downwards
and stamping upwards. Then as he came out on
top of a rise, panting and gasping, his face contorted by the collecting panic, he halted. His eyes
started from his head, his squint crossing horrific-
ally. He threw back his head and barrelling his
chest he bellowed.

'Sionnach!'

Out of the heathers some yards away a handful

of blackcock started and flew in terror round the corner of the hill. On his left a small waterfall splashed over the rocks. Up above, the sky was a thin blue sail holed here and there by clouds.

Alasdair stayed implanted in the ground, legs like young tree trunks, fists still clenched, his whole body quivering. His face, twisted by thought, might have been an image of pain. For years his life had been one of peace and small pleasures with the land and now he felt himself exposed to a threat from outside. And his desire was to root out this threat, to chase it away. . . .

But gradually the tension dissolved. The moment passed. And he saw himself once again on the land with nothing but the hills and animals about him and the flat sheets of the sea and sky beyond. He had held to the life he knew for all these years through all the rigours of solitude and he could not envisage an end. Neither man nor storm would drive him from his home. And, all of a sudden, An Sionnach's threat was nothing to him.

He started on his way again, calmer now but still disturbed. His heavy boots trod the single-track path that wriggled its way through heathers and brackens, sometimes climbing a short way on to the hill to avoid a marsh, sometimes vanishing into the bones of rocky ground.

And now he was walking as he always walked on his return to Cragaig. There was the extra spring in his toes at each step which propelled him homewards with unaccustomed speed; there was also the silent gleam of hope and expectation in his complicated eyes. And there was no drudge in this walk; it was a mission of deep affection which made the obstacles of hill and heathers shrink before the power of this man's step.

As this pinprick wove across the plaid of the moors the day was already well past its prime. The sun was still up but was fast aiming for the western rim of the sea and the light had begun to soften. The spinning orb of the sun had started to take on the pinkness of decline as if an internal wound was leaking out across its surface and with this the sharp outlines of the coast were melting. The braes of coarse grass with their scabs of heathers and brackens were being transformed. The heathers and brackens which had stood out under a metallic finish in the midday light were now sinking to mottlings of rust and dried blood while the grasses, blanched and old, took on the colour of faded pearls. High in the sky above some distant rocks an eagle turned ever slowly, the underside of its immense wingspan lit up by the light from across the sea.

Alasdair rose out of the last dip and reached the crest of the hill behind Cragaig. Already the outside world seemed distant; the conversation about An Sionnach unreal. There below was the centre of his life and out beyond, the ever shifting surface of the sea, his daily companion in work. A mile or two from the shore a small fishing-boat headed for home, its prow high out of the water and pushing an ermine streamer as it ploughed northwards.

The house below stood still. The animals grazed peacefully, only the hens disturbing the stillness as they jerked and pecked about the ground. Alasdair stretched and once again was pleased.

5

DOWN in the village, Alasdair busied himself in
the evening meeting with his animals. He found
new joy in his conversation with them, new
friendship with his soft-eyed cow. When he milked
her that still, crisping evening the song which
wound out of his throat seemed to suck out the
last residues of bile which lay in his soul from the
afternoon. The melancholy of the opening in-
tonation, a cry from the distant past, evolved
into a growing fit of elation. Somewhere deep
inside Alasdair's being there lay unharmed the
berry of hope, that illogical giver of faith and joy
in the face of even the cruellest setbacks. There
was little in Alasdair Mór's life which could have
given reason to rejoice in the expectation of a
better future—indeed, all he had to look forward
to was an ever increasingly difficult existence
and a painful old age. And yet such was the
warmth and closeness he felt for the country and
animals of Cragaig that every now and again the
deepest quarters of his soul would erupt in a
quiet passion. Here in this muted milking song
his soul, in spite of himself and his usual inarti-
culateness, flowered in shaking quarter-tones and
great shifting pedal notes which lay like threads

entwined within the intricate weavings of the burn
and distant surf.

He milked slowly, trying to prolong the moments of oblivion, his eyes now wide, now half-
closed, his head tilting back and then coming
slowly forward to rest on the cow's flank where he
felt the softness and pulsing warmth of the
creature against the sliding rhythms of the chant.
His cold forehead pressed into the thick red coat,
his hairy nose inhaling all the scents of earthy
life, richer to him than all the concoctions of man.
Then he rolled his head to the left so that his ear
was against the cow's side, and he heard, as the
vague pluckings and rollings of a thorough-bass,
the intestinal movements of the beast.

Perhaps this scene was re-enacted twice a day
but it never lost its wild charms for Alasdair and
on this occasion after the turmoils in his mind
earlier in the afternoon, it took on a rare passion.
Not often before had the sheep and hens and the
circling buzzard seen the man quiver and tremble
so, not often had they heard his voice crack and
strain under the effects of such joy. And they
came towards him as the plant comes towards the
sun. The hens jerked and strutted in a ring about
him and the cow; the sheep stood lined up on the
crest of a slope above and stayed there frozen in
fascination; and birds of all kinds collected in
levels and stacks about the village. Gulls and
hoodies turned and stalled in the lower airs above
the cow; blackbirds and thrushes rose out of no-

where and cast sidelong glances down on this strange scene; a kestrel hovered; a pair of buzzards wheeled high, crying out like despondent children.

When it was all over and the creatures had dispersed, Alasdair felt the need to stay out for a while longer in the open air and having shut up his hens he made his way across the village grass, past the top of the garden and up on to the hillock.

On top of the hillock the heathers grew in profusion. They grew thick and deep as a man's knees and the browning purple of the dying flowers lay like wild grains scattered on the surface of a turbulent sea. Here Alasdair stopped and sat himself down, the springy depths of the heathers acting as insulation from the cold ground beneath. He sat there like a bird in a covert, only the top half of him showing, the rest buried deep in the quiltings of the ground.

The peace in his mind was supreme. It was a peace which was based on no practical considerations but which rose from a strange ability to find his balance in relation to the world. For most men it is something which can only last briefly after which they slip back to the insecurities and buried worries of their daily existence. For Alasdair it was an experience which moved ceaselessly in and out of his life carrying him along on a level which had little to do with that of the outside world. And for Alasdair, that evening, the sensation was that of the hawk hovering, the loss of the perspectives of time. And the sea before him, stretching out like a breastplate of polished steel with the great road of light from the foundered sun upon it, the sea also reflected the calm within him.

He looked northwards and saw the hills rise and then fall steeply in the cliffs to the beaches. And the winter sunlight's pink skein caught on these slopes like tangle on a reef. And behind the shelves and gradients of light the half shadows, terrible bruises on soft flesh, and the full shadows in the ravines and gullets like dribbles of thick black ink.

He looked southwards and saw cliffs again and from behind them the indistinct shape of the island of Risga with its long western promontory fingering the Atlantic in the winter haze. Out beyond Risga the horizon had disappeared in the haze so that sea and sky seemed to have merged into one.

Alasdair sat in the heathers for a while and then, on a sudden impulse, levered himself to his feet and wandered off over the hillock to the edge of the cliff. He shambled along sniffing at the air with its new winter smoky smells, rubbing his hands together for warmth and out of satisfaction.

He came down to the edge of the cliff where the winds had worn away the turf and exposed the crumbling rock. He came down to it cautiously for the soft rock was treacherous. And there

on the edge a new panorama opened. From
further back on the hill he had seen only the
distant sea, a flat shiny plain with no dimensions
other than infinity. But here he was greeted by the
metallic hiss of the surf, by a slight breeze, by the
contours of the coast which lent proportion to the
sea.

His eyes wandered up along the coast picking
out the distant spots of his buoys. Then back
down the coast beneath him and along to the
mouth of the burn. The mouth of the burn!
By Christ! At the mouth of the burn a small
boat bobbed, its oars flapping in the breathing
of the swell and a man leaning over the gunwale
was hauling in a creel line.

The light was already too dim to make out any
details of the man, but Alasdair, for a moment,
did not think to wonder who it might be. It was
just another man, some bastard who was hauling
in his, Alasdair Mór's, own line. Lifting his very
own creels, his best creels, rebuilt with loving
care. And on his best ground. To work another
man's creels was the one unforgivable crime among
the lobstermen.

All this in the first half of a split second. Then,
in the other half, realisation, recognition.

'An Sionnach, the bugger!'

Alasdair could easily have shouted a threat, a
curse at the man, but that would have warned
him and he would have dropped the line and fled
long before Alasdair could get anywhere near

him. And Alasdair wanted to get near him, to pay him in full for his deed.

But Alasdair found himself rooted to the spot. A sort of dull fascination held him there, forcing him to watch the scene develop. Part of him was unbelieving, incredulous that anyone, least of all a neighbour, should dare this insult to him, under his very nose, in daylight. He watched the spider of a man, a small monochrome blob, arms swimming as he pulled in the long line hand over hand. He watched the black frames of his prize creels surface from the water and the man starting to reach and grope into them. Only then, like a delayed charge, did Alasdair move.

And how he moved! He span on his heels, his arms stretched out in balance, his face frozen in the distortions of anger. From the cliff to the village was a matter of a few stag-like bounds, clearing the heathers with unimagined agility. He almost broke down the door of his house with the speed of his arrival. He thrust a handful of bullets into his pocket, seized his rifle and burst out of the building again. From the village along the cliff top he sprinted and bounded, his customary pigeon-toed stepping put aside for the crashing of mighty strides. The ground trembled beneath the thundering of his boots, the brackens parted before the blast of air that he pushed in front of him and birds rose from the heathers and grass at the sound of this maddened creature approaching.

'The wee cunt! the wee cunt!' It was the fact
of his finally having set eyes on An Sionnach that
had dispelled the tremulous anxiety which he had
felt with regard to his neighbour. Now the animal
instincts of this great man, untapped over forty-
five years, had suddenly burst forth in an un-
inhibited torrent and he ceaselessly mouthed
short explosions of abuse as he ran, which acted as
a safety valve to the growing pressure of fury
within him.

He came to the top of the path down the cliff
and scarcely halted before the steep descent.
Rather he leaped out into space, windmilled his
arms to retain his balance and came crunching
down on the rocky surface of the path below.
A moment's pause of adjustment and the left
leg kicked forward into the next bound.

He was transfigured. The black hate of the
first minutes had changed into a look of serene
determination. His eyes were wide, steady, flam-
ing with a passionate belief in his inner anger.
And his limbs, usually so painfully uncoordinated
and clumsy, took on the harnessed strength of an
athlete.

He ski'd down a long stretch of loose rocks,
holding the rifle before him in both hands, stamped hard on a solid piece of ground and took off
again into a plummeting fall to a lower section of
the path and so missing out a long hairpin bend.
Another sharp corner and this time he failed to
hold his course. He tried to slow down and turn,

half succeeded and then fell forward over the edge of the track, gasping and cursing as he went. He dropped the rifle and it went slithering down the slope. He turned a complete somersault in mid-air, saw the inverted horizon way above him and landed on his back on a section of steep grass. A great puff of air was expelled from his lungs by the impact. But with the steepness of the cliff and his momentum the top half of his body followed through and with all the skill of a professional tumbler he came out of the fall on his feet and bounded away again like a goat. A few feet lower down he stooped and picked up his rifle in mid-stride and flew onwards.

He passed through bracken and heather in his descent, scorning the path where it twisted backwards and forwards on the grass, and came out like a savage from the bush with knotted ferns and heather sprigs tangling round his thighs and crutch. Only when he came to the last yards of the cliff where a short stretch of springy grass joined it to the upper beach did he release the grip on himself so that he just let himself fall and roll and tumble and slither downwards. And as soon as he came to rest on the field he jumped to his feet and set off again towards the little harbour.

When he arrived he dropped the rifle into the bows of the boat, seized the oars, half fell, half jumped into the boat and with feverish, fumbling fingers slipped the rope and pushed off. In his eagerness he began to row too soon, bringing the left oar down with a resounding thwack on the jetty stones but a second later he was clear and pulling hard for open water. He bent his back into the oars so that the wood under his grasp almost creaked with the pressure of his grip and the shafts themselves seemed to bow from the force of his strokes.

By now, the light was thickening, but as he cleared the harbour a quick glance over his shoulder told him that the other boat was still on the creels at the mouth of the burn. The man—the cursed man—was bent, working in the bottom of the boat, unaware of the raging force that was skimming up on him across the surface of the sea.

Now Alasdair left off cursing and fell silent, only grunting with effort to the count of his rowing. He knew, too, that he must move quietly as well as swiftly if he were to catch An Sionnach. But there was still the distance of half a mile between them and his plan presupposed that An Sionnach would not keep a lookout as he worked. By now An Sionnach was lifting the second set of Alasdair's creels at the mouth of the burn and still appeared to be quite unaware of his danger. And as Alasdair moved swiftly and silently on over the water there was a great chain of questions and half-questions running through his mind which fused with his anger and lent him strength.

Again, as earlier in the day, he asked himself

why this stranger should have taken against him.
Why, from one unlucky night when the man had
suffered a serious setback with the loss of his
creels and when he, Alasdair, had had the good
fortune to get by almost unscathed, should he
have vowed some sort of vengeance? And what
sort of vengeance was this? To steal his lobsters.
An Sionnach, wherever he came from, must have
known what happened to men caught red-handed
at somebody else's creels. Alasdair remembered
one of the rare cases of this happening on the
island, some years back.

The culprit, a man called MacVicar, who had
fallen on hard times, had decided to try his luck.
For a week or two he had succeeded for the men
whose creels he was working had not managed to
catch him at it. But the men were sure it was he
for he had been seen on their part of the coast
too often for mere coincidence. Well, finally
exasperated, maddened by the thief's nerve and
by the inevitable loss of money, the lobstermen
banded together and laid a plan to catch him.

Four men had stationed themselves in a boat
on the south side of a headland while two others
on the cliffs had kept watch on the coast to the
north of the headland, where the creels were set.
Sure enough, an hour or two later, MacVicar had
put out in a small boat from an inlet just up the
coast and had started down towards the creels.
The lookouts had let him begin to raise the first
creels and had then hurried across the headland to

give the signal to the men in the boat below. Immediately this boat, with two strong men at the oars and two others ready in the stern, had put out round the point and borne down on MacVicar.

Two days later, by chance, a fishing boat on its way home to one of the mainland ports to the south had seen a boat drifting a mile or two out to sea. They turned from their course to investigate and found young MacVicar lying in the bottom of the boat. There were no oars, no signs of provisions, nothing apart from the semi-conscious MacVicar who proved to have three cracked ribs, a broken arm and a shattered jaw. By some good fortune the weather had not broken during the hours he had drifted down the coast but even so his condition was serious, both from his wounds and exposure. The fishermen washed the caked blood from his bruised face and put him ashore in the south of the island where an old woman took him in and cared for him. Six weeks later when his body had recovered, he thanked the woman and took the first boat over to the mainland, not even going back to his bothy to collect his belongings. And MacVicar had never been seen on the island since. . . . An Sionnach must know what he was risking.

The light had dimmed even more. When Alasdair next paused and glanced round to see what An Sionnach was doing he could no longer distinguish colours and shadings. An Sionnach and the dipping boat were flattened to two-dimensional shapes. But what Alasdair could see was that An Sionnach was moving about as if he had finished with the lobsters and was preparing to head for home. And there was still a good three hundred yards between the two boats.

For a minute or two more Alasdair continued to row towards An Sionnach. Then, he heard the clatter and splash of the creels being thrown overboard and as he turned to look An Sionnach swung his boat round and caught sight of Alasdair.

For a brief moment the two men sat looking at each other and then Alasdair hurled himself back on his oars, mouthing uncontrolled abuse. He now realised that An Sionnach was going to escape him and the imminent thwarting of his plans roused him to another peak of fury.

That wind-scored face of his, with its wandering eyes and its great fleshy nose in between, that coarse skin with its wild clusters of sprouting hairs, those sea-fruit lips—all that which lay beneath the parapet of his greasy old cap became ferocious. For those few seconds when he believed that a mad spurt of rowing could still get him to An Sionnach, Alasdair Mór's face was that of a wild beast. His breath came like the rootings of a pig. An enormously swollen vein crept out from beneath his cap, slid across his temple and vanished into his hair. As he finished each stroke of the oars he half rose off the seat such was the suddenly inordinate strength in his arms.

But try as he might he would not be able to

make up the two hundred and fifty yards that separated him from his quarry. For An Sionnach too was bending his oars against the thole-pins in an attempt to maintain the distance between the two boats. Alasdair kept up the pressure for another few minutes and then, quite suddenly realising that he would soon lose An Sionnach in the approaching darkness, he stopped rowing, dropped the oars and stood up. He turned and saw the hazy outline of An Sionnach rowing frenetically away down the coast.

'Sionnach, ye wee bastard!' For the second time that day Alasdair bellowed this name in a state of paroxysmal anger. Against the grey light of the sky Alasdair's profile was that of an eagle, features fierce and beady, head thrust forward, arms and clenched fists pushed back against the oars like aerodynamic wings.

But the man kept rowing as if he had not heard Alasdair. In the poor light it looked as if the boat were stationary and the oars just flapping up and down helplessly like the wings of a young fulmar. But the boat was in fact moving fast, making sure that a good distance was kept between it and Alasdair.

Alasdair shouted again and this time the man stopped rowing. Whether he thought the distance between them was now safe enough or whether he was putting his trust in the gathering dusk was not clear but he stopped rowing and sat there half leaning on the oars.

'Sionnach!' Alasdair's voice rang out like a double-edged sword in the murk. Silence. A small flurry of wind fluttered in Alasdair's seaward ear.

'Sionnach! I ken well enough that it's ye. Ye wee bugger! if I catch ye again within sight of my creels I'll kill ye!' Alasdair stopped suddenly, hoping to have spurred An Sionnach into declaring himself. He wanted to hear this phantom's voice, wanted to hear him answer to his name.

He waited half a minute or so, his eyes piercing the gloom to see what the man was doing. But the man was doing nothing. Just sitting there waiting. With a curse Alasdair leapt to his oars again and set off once more in pursuit. But immediately, An Sionnach followed suit and once again the boats moved down the coast in formation. Again Alasdair stopped and shouted and, getting no reply, set off again. And again An Sionnach did as before. Finally Alasdair stood up and shouted, telling An Sionnach to stop running like the coward he was. At this An Sionnach also stood up and the two men stood there in their boats on the shifting waters. Taut strands of silence held them at this prescribed distance.

When An Sionnach twice more refused to react to Alasdair's threats and taunts, Alasdair grimly decided that the man needed teaching a lesson. He seized the rifle from the bows, pushed a round into the breech, released the safety catch and took aim. An Sionnach never moved. Puzzled, Alasdair lowered the rifle and frowned. Was the bugger mad? Did he want to be shot? Well, by Christ, he'd get what he wanted then.

He raised the rifle again, took aim and fired. The explosion splintered the evening silence, the almost electrical sharpness of the sound hammering off cliff and rock. But with the light almost gone and the combination of the rocking boat and Alasdair's hand shaking with fury, the shot, at a distance of some three hundred yards, went wide. The whine of the bullet coiled off into the gloom. And An Sionnach never moved. He stood there as ever, insolent, monstrous.

In all, Alasdair fired five rounds. He might have been shooting at a tin can for target practice for all that An Sionnach moved. One of the shots must have hit the boat for there was the sound of impact and splintering wood. But even then An Sionnach never moved.

Finally, in despair at his marksmanship, Alasdair cast the rifle aside and just stood there staring at the slowly vanishing profile of his target.

The violence of the five explosions in the evening air and the vicious kick of the butt on his shoulder had done something to alleviate the tension which had held his mind and body so fiercely. Now, with the unreality of the situation, he slumped down on the seat, rested his elbows on his knees and gazed over the water to where the other boat continued to wallow with its statue-like occupant. The mad action of the previous

95

hour dissolved into the gauzy quality of a dream.

Time passed. Then An Sionnach suddenly turned away and sat down. He picked up his oars and calmly began to row away into the gloom. Alasdair sat and watched, unmoved. A couple of minutes later An Sionnach's boat was no longer to be seen.

Alasdair stayed where he was, perched on the movement of the sea that swung as a rocking cradle to his mind. As he reflected on the whole matter, he found it strange, so strange indeed that he wondered momentarily if he had not imagined part of it. There was no doubt that somebody had been working his creels; and there was no doubt in his mind that somebody had been An Sionnach. But had An Sionnach really just sat there and watched him without making his get-away as speedily and furtively as the normal thief would have done? And, strangest of all, had he simply stood there in his boat while Alasdair had loaded and fired five times? The man, for all the thief he was, must indeed be an odd one. For no common man, even in pitch darkness, stands stock still while rifle bullets whine past him. Who was this man An Sionnach? Where was he from? What were his motives against him? The whole matter, right from the meeting with Aulay, was too much for Alasdair's brain. No matter which way he looked at it he could not begin to fathom out this man.

Alasdair shivered. The sweat had left a skin of

chill on his flesh. His eyes mechanically watched a small cloud of mad-headed lapwings bank and curve its way over the shore. A few minutes later a large fish broke the surface near the boat and then headed away into the depths for the night. A slight breeze ruffled the surface waters and flustered round Alasdair's ears. He shivered again. Then, as if rising from a pit of sleep, he straightened up and looked about. Already the mid-distance was thick with the coal-dust of night and it was only with difficulty that he could make out the silhouettes of the coast. He ought to be getting home.

He spun himself slowly round on the seat and took hold of the oars. With a few deft strokes he turned the boat and quickly settled into a steady pace up the coast.

The two scaup which winged their way with eager necks northwards over the shallow water saw nothing but the grainy form of a man rowing slowly home in the dusk. They saw him pull time and again in strict rhythm without once raising his eyes from the stern of the boat. They saw the boat and its man move a few yards up the coast as they passed overhead and then, as he slipped from their sight, they forgot him and thought only of the thick aquatic plants which lay below the waters of the bay to which they were heading. What they did not see was the weighty slowness of his shoulder muscles as he worked at the oars; nor did they see the tired and baffled expression on his face beneath the peaked cap. The forehead wrinkled, the eyebrows diving together in a knot, the eyes small and pained, the mouth stretched in the man's macabre, grin-like thinking posture.

Alasdair felt that his life had been put to rout. He felt his daily routine from over the years scattered by the arrival of this mad foreigner who seemed to know neither fear nor sense. He felt himself unjustly attacked, harassed, and saw the beginnings of a life in which stealth and secrecy were major factors. He, Alasdair Mór! He who had never hidden anything from anybody in all his years at Cragaig. That he should start the hiding and watching, the waiting and guarding of a local, bitter war. . . . And so in the fevered complications of an exhausted and edgy mind, Alasdair Mór's worries multiplied and proliferated.

At Port nam Freumh he secured the boat and walked away into the darkness. Half-way up the cliff path he had to stop and sit down on a rock. For five minutes he stayed there, cocooned in the cold and dark, quite suddenly overcome by despair. Alasdair Mór was experiencing new and fearful things.

Later, he sighed deeply, stood up and started out once again on the ever steepening road to his home.

6

FOR the week or two following An Sionnach's raid on Alasdair's creels the weather held. There were days when the cold blue sky drew slightly back to let in a layer of thick dirty cloud between it and the air of the sea lands, but never once did anything more than a breeze worry the water, never once did a drop of rain fall. Aulay said that it was no canny, that this was the time of year for the winds and rain, that they would be getting a terrible time of it after the New Year. But Alasdair was not bothered by the way the weather was holding. On the contrary, as each dawn came calm and cold, he would breathe a sigh of relief and go to sea again for another day on the creels. While this still weather lasted the lobsters might stay in the shallower coastal waters where Alasdair could fish them. And he fished feverishly, often lifting his creels several times a day, for he knew that once the winds came, bringing heavy seas with them, the lobsters would move out to their winter grounds in deep water. And there the seas would give Alasdair little chance of working.

Right into the second week of November he was able to work to this routine. Up in the dark,

he would stumble around heavy-eyed in the weak
light of the paraffin lamp, getting his breakfast
and patting some stale pieces of bread round
dried dulse and cheese for his lunch. Then in the
waning darkness he would be out to milk the
cow and tend to the other animals before setting
off for Port nam Freumh. Once at the harbour he
would fill his box with bait and be pulling the
boat clear of the coast by the time the sun rose
from behind the hills and sent its first light
diving out over the long stretching shadows to
touch the far-away sea in a hive of sparks. From
then until sunset he would work his way up and
down the coast, periodically lifting the creels and
filling in time in between by fishing with a line
from the boat. Sitting there in his drifting boat,
Alasdair caught cod, whiting, cuddies, mackerel
and dogfish. He would lay aside a couple of
cuddies for his supper and then throw the rest of
the catch into the box of bait. With the setting of
the sun he was back on land and making his way
home.

But then, one morning—the morning of Martin-
mas—Alasdair awoke to hear the stirrings of a
wind. By the time he had done the milking the
half-light was there and Alasdair could see by the
running clouds and the whipped tops of the
waves rolling in from the open sea that the calm
spell had broken. He made straight for Port nam
Freumh and within the hour had all his creels
in. Even so, he was taking a buffeting by the time

he reached the harbour again for the wind was increasing steadily. But the creels were in so there was no worry and all he could do now was to wait and see how the weather developed.

The clouds crowded the sky as they jostled in from over the horizon like frightened birds before a great fire. Beneath them the rows of waves came ceaselessly across the sea, crests whitened here and there by the pluckings of a swirling surface wind, to throw up their long-contained power on the rocks of the shore. As the wind-sent waters approached the coast they met the rising shoals and shelvings and so rose in height till it seemed impossible that with their curled white fringes they should go another yard without falling head first before their own feet. And yet they did. They ran onwards like jugglers, holding their crests on the very limit of equilibrium so that their momentum was multiplied greatly in the last yards of their life. Then, at last, the shore was in reach and with a final effort they drew back their heads, paused and cast themselves down on the land.

They burst in a thousand different ways—some with spite, some with thundering hate, some with delicate glee, some simply with relief—but they all cast great blankets of spume and salt milk over the black boulders and outcrops of rock. Sometimes the surf enclosed the rocks in explosions of water and air so that the area was temporarily obscured and by the time the atmosphere cleared

the water was fast draining away. At other times–
when a wave broke prematurely–the bubbling
surf ran up over the flatter rocks like young
sheep escaping over a wall. And then arms,
fingers, nails of foam were up and into cracks and
crevices, holes, creases, tunnels, caves so that the
sullen block of rock was quite suddenly alive with
running, twisting life. But then, the momentum
died and the rushing waters slowed, halted and
began to fall, to be sucked and dragged backwards into the mouth of the following wave.

The whole coast–as far as the eye could see–
was bordered with this shaking fleece. Alasdair
rubbed his knees together, shifted the haft of the
great fish knife which lay tucked into his belt and
gazed out to sea. From where he stood, at the top
of the path from Port nam Freumh, the waves
stretched into the dim middle distance where
they were lost in the hazy confusion between
sea and sky. And the wind which drove these
waves, left them at the land's edge and hurried
upwards towards the hills. It came up the gullets
with a roaring and boring, tearing at the hardy
plant life and knotting the stalks of bracken into
nests of tangles. At the lip of the cliff it caught
the waters of sea-hunting burns and foiled them
by lifting every drop upwards in a pillar and
casting them back on to the land. Looking along
the coast Alasdair saw the smoke of numbers of
these cliff-top fires.

But now he turned away and started to walk

towards the village. There was no sign of a break in the weather and there was little he could do except wait.

When he got back to Cragaig, he threw his piece-bag into the corner, whetted his knife on the stone, and picking up an old sack, set off out of the village to collect some kindling. As most of the driftwood on the beach was too large he headed southwards along the cliffs to a spot where a cluster of birch trees grew. The storm which had cost An Sionnach his creels had also brought down a couple of these trees and although their stunted growth did not afford much solid wood the twigs and small branches had grown in a weird sort of profusion. These, if left to dry, gave a poor kind of kindling. In the matter of the natural amenities of survival, the headland was not overgenerous.

Alasdair walked fast, skirting the edge of the cliff and feeling the wind slapping at his seaward cheek. When he crossed a burn he received a sharp spraying from the water as it failed to make the plunge to the sea and was lifted briskly skywards. He rolled along, seemingly impelled by an irresistible force, each shoulder dropping exaggeratedly in time with his boot on the same side striking the ground—just as if he had never learned how to walk.

And as he walked, his polished eyes wandered about him in their madness so that he scarcely watched where he was going. Instead he saw the small forms of the pipits, the cocked shape of a dipper along the edge of the burn, the small flock of snow buntings undulating through the air towards the open hillside. Further back from the edge of the cliff he stopped to examine a deer's slot. It appeared to interest him for he looked at it carefully and then glanced up sharply and scanned the hill.

He passed the point of Rudha na Leap and was just about to cut back inland to the birch trees when something on the shore below caught his eye. Right down by the water, standing on a large promontory of rock, were two people. A man and a woman. The man, from what Alasdair knew of him, resembled An Sionnach.

Alasdair stopped. An Sionnach, with his back to the sea, was shouting furiously at the woman. She, a tall strong-looking woman, stood facing him, her head lowered, more in defence than submission. Her dark hair was gathered behind her head in a bun and revealed a white neck. That and the two small patches of white which were her hands were all that showed of her. The rest lay beneath a long-sleeved dress of dark blue material.

They stood there, the man shouting. Occasionally a cloud of light spray was thrown up by the surf below but neither of them flinched as it covered them. Alasdair wondered if the woman were silent all this time or whether she was answering the man. But he could not tell for she never

raised her head nor made any gesture. Whatever her reactions were An Sionnach appeared to
pause every now and again and wait for her to
say something before he launched into a new
attack.

From time to time the wind carried An Sionnach's voice up to Alasdair as he stood perched
on the edge of the cliff but he could make nothing
of what he heard. On and on An Sionnach appeared to rave, as if out of control and then, quite
suddenly, he turned away from her in exasperation. She never moved. He, the while, was
kicking at loose pebbles and rubbing the back of
his neck. Then he tired of this too and turned
towards the land again, carefully ignoring the
woman, who still stood motionless before him.
An Sionnach was casting his eyes about when he
caught sight of Alasdair's form up on the cliffs.
He must then have said something for the
woman suddenly looked up at him as if in surprise. She saw him staring over her shoulder
and slowly turned to follow his gaze.

At that distance it was difficult to make out
any details. Even with his hawk-like eyesight
Alasdair saw no more than an open, white face
and hair gathered from a central parting like
looped curtains in a window. He saw too, in her
movement of turning, the intimation of broad
shoulders and the line of a full breast. But
though he could see little of her what Alasdair
noticed was the way she kept her eyes on him.

And under her gaze he found himself forgetting to watch An Sionnach, found himself straining his sight into the gale to see more of this woman of whom he knew nothing beyond her boldness.

His eyes were watering and he blinked. Still the three people stood motionless out on the shores of that distant headland. Alasdair, mouth slightly open, scratched his stubbly cheek with the back of his hand. But his watery, squinting eyes did not seem to notice this intrusion. Nor did he notice when a herring gull, caught by a rising current of air, rose swiftly within a few feet of his face. Inexplicably, he was being drawn forward from the narrow confines of his awareness. He felt that he wanted to look away yet continued to gaze. He trembled. He realised too that he was intruding, that he had been caught eavesdropping and thought that he should perhaps walk on. And yet he stayed.

Then An Sionnach moved and said something to the woman. She, without turning fully, replied, held her position as if waiting for an answer and then turned to face An Sionnach. For a moment Alasdair was forgotten as the woman stood, head high, proudly facing An Sionnach. The latter appeared to be beside himself with rage. He stood there, fists clenched, leaning slightly forward, shaking, unable to speak. The woman turned away, walked across to the other side of the neck of rock and looked back at Alasdair. And again her eyes held him. He found himself watching her

with a helpless fascination. But this lasted only a
few seconds. For An Sionnach suddenly sprang
forward, raised an arm and brought it down
viciously on the side of the woman's neck. She
never heard him coming and went down as if
poleaxed. She crumpled like a rag doll and went
backwards off the rock into the surf.

An Sionnach watched her fall, saw her hit the
water and then started to walk away down the
coast.

When An Sionnach struck the woman Alasdair
started from his trance. He breathed a curse and
headed forward to a point where the cliff rose less
high. He dropped the sack and began to make his
way down the steep slope. As he ran, bumping and
hopping in his own peculiar style, he cast occasional glances in the direction of the shore but of
the woman there was nothing to be seen. The
surf broke ceaselessly on the rock, the backwash
of each wave running into the following breaker.

Alasdair knew that the rocks fell steeply on this
part of the coast and that with the tide being
high the water would have a bad depth to it. And
he imagined the weight of the long dress full of
water and shuddered. He feared for the woman.

When he came out on the upper beach there
was still no sign of her. Nor was there of An
Sionnach who had vanished round an outcrop in
the cliff a few hundred yards down the coast.
For a moment, as he moved forward into the
turmoils of the wind, Alasdair wondered if his

imagination had not been playing tricks on him. Perhaps he had stood alone on that coast. Perhaps the man and woman had been illusions in his watering eyes. For, indeed, queer things had been happening to him of late. And yet he hurried on to the shore where there was nothing but the storm wind and the bundling sea.

But as he came nearer to the rocks he saw something move. A rounded outline, which at a glance might have been taken for a smooth rock, showed against the sea. It remained still for a few seconds then again it began to shift, to rise so that Alasdair knew it as the back of the woman climbing on hands and knees from the sea. He hurried forward.

However, when he was some hundred paces from her, she suddenly rose clear of the rocks and stood up. Alasdair halted, once again aware that he was intruding, that he might not be wanted. His mouth twisted and turned as he bit at his lower lip; his right hand scratched at his thigh; he shuffled his feet.

The woman stood there, swaying slightly and breathing heavily. A gash on her forehead dribbled blood so that it mingled with sea water and traced a number of different paths down on to her right cheek and neck. Her thick dark-brown hair now hung in confusion almost to her waist. Using both hands she pushed it back off her face and shoulders. This gesture pulled at the upper half of her dress, tautening the sea-drenched material so

that from between the flattened forms of her
large breasts a small trickle of water was pressed.
She dropped her arms to her side and stood there
panting, looking straight at Alasdair.

Her skin was white, now overlaid with a waxen
chill. But it was her eyes that he noticed first.
The colour of black-brown earth. The garden at
Cragaig. With an uncanny stillness to them. Even
as she stood there panting, exhausted by her
struggle in the icy sea, her eyes never flickered but
held Alasdair in their gaze. And also a strangely
prominent upper lip, slightly bulging over
closely packed teeth. With this and the breadth
of her jaw, the whole of her face seemed bottom-
heavy. A small pear. With lips of fruit-fleshness.

She stood tall, perhaps only a hand's breadth
shorter than Alasdair himself, with broad shoulders and the suggestion of fatted strength in her
upper arms beneath the clinging skin of her dress.
Alasdair thought vaguely of her kneading a
bowlful of wholemeal dough. But the shape of her
hands was oddly delicate for a crofter's woman.
She moved her fingers continuously to regain the
circulation. Fronds of dulse through a clear sea.
From her waist, her body grew out again to hips
and legs of strength.

There on that desolate stretch of foreshore with
an Atlantic storm running in on the land and the
waves casting veils of spume high into the air,
Alasdair and the woman stood as if transfixed.
Alasdair's nervous twitchings had long since fallen

still and he stood, braced against the wind, his
mind in a turmoil of puzzled excitement. He was
hardly aware that she was looking at him for he
was too taken up with looking at her. He examined her minutely, shamelessly but quite without salaciousness, as a farmer looks appraisingly
at a well proportioned beast. And yet while he
took in all the details of her body it was to her
face that his eyes kept returning, the face with a
strangely enigmatic expression. His first impression was that the woman was angry with him.
Her face was set, her eyes fixed in a manner
which told him to beware. But as he looked he
saw in her deep, still eyes that she was frightened.
But if she was frightened why did she stand there,
why did she not turn home? There was, to
Alasdair's mind, a queerness in it.

For a few minutes longer they stood watching
each other. Alasdair, for all his usual shyness,
now found himself at ease, so consumed was he
by this strange woman who feared him yet did
not run. He had temporarily stepped out of the
constrictions of his normal behaviour. He just
stood and gazed. But he was disconcerted by the
fear which he saw in the woman's eyes. The
uncomprehending fear of a young animal. He
wanted to explain that he meant no harm. He
took a step forward.

The woman started, suddenly brought to her
senses by the movement, shook back her hair in a
defiant gesture, looked Alasdair straight in the

face with stern eyes, turned on her heel and walked away.

Of a sudden the wind leapt with a muscular spring, lifting spray and light surf in a dense cloud, part of which fell on Alasdair with a stinging force even at that distance from the sea. He blinked at the sudden impact, then blinked again slowly twice more, moving his eyes to clear his vision. The woman was walking away. Seen from behind, her dark-blue form moved like a magnificent boat riding the rough grasses of the shore. She swayed and rose over the tussocks and mounds, the small muscles of her shoulders and back clenching and lying beneath the wet garments. Mackerel spines. As she walked, the irregularity of the ground caused her hips to move in an ever changing pendulum rhythm pivoting from the small of her back. Beneath the long flowing skirt the suggestion was one of firmness, sweet waterskins, while her legs were born of a strength of the hills. Every few paces her hands pushed her hair away from her face and the movement was the shaping of a mid-ocean wave. The diamond of her raised arms exposing the sides and flesh of her lower body. Soft and vulnerable and half known. She seemed a creature streaked with effortless guile and genuine innocence. The woman.

Alasdair frowned and rubbed his eye with the joint of his thumb. He looked away far out to sea and his face puckered before the wind. But he soon looked back again to watch the woman until she disappeared round the angle in the cliff. When she had gone, Alasdair was left with the wind and the waves blowing in on the land in a changeless procession of energies. He stood there, quite still, watching the distant shore and finding a comfort in the sea-wind as it ran over and about him.

For some minutes further he did not move. He stayed with his eyes fixed on the same spot, way down the shore, where nothing now stirred except the grasses under the currents of air. He seemed to be watching something but there was nothing in particular to see. Or to be waiting for something but nothing happened. He saw nothing, expected nothing and yet was unable to take his eyes from the small corner of the landscape which had blotted out the woman. An Sionnach's woman. And what was An Sionnach's woman to Alasdair Mór? He himself could not formulate an answer to this. In that hour of his life a woman had stood alone before him for a few moments and then disappeared. A chance encounter and no more. And yet this encounter had done something to him. He felt jolted, out of step; the rigid panels of his life broken into. He, the great bull of a man, was disarmed. That day on the shore beyond Rudha na Leap, Alasdair Mór's peace of mind was sorely disturbed by An Sionnach's woman.

At last he moved. Slowly, as if painfully, he

broke himself out of his stance on the grass, saw again the tangling herring gulls searching the shore and the Achateny sheep head down to their grazing. And as he saw them he awoke to the fact that his life was not changed, that it would go on just as before with the weeks and months of featureless routine. That he was nothing to the woman, that the woman belonged to An Sionnach, a man who had sworn himself a threat to Alasdair. As he walked back towards the cliff his common-sense told him all this yet the restlessness, the flurries that ran in his heart stood out against his better judgement.

In order to obliterate the disturbance in his mind he lengthened his stride and made hastily for the bottom of the cliff. As he started to climb, he drove himself up the steep slope as fast as he could, forcing his body onwards without respite. He came out on top breathing heavily, dizzy from the effort. But straightaway he turned inland and, picking up the sack, made for the little group of birch trees below the hill.

Here he set to work on the twigs and smaller branches of a tree that lay canted against a rock. He used his powerful hands where the wood was thin enough to snap and then slashed furiously at the greener, large branches. He worked fast, never stopping for a moment, keeping his mind on the job in hand until the sack was full. Eventually it was no longer possible to cram another stick into the sack. He thrust the knife back into the sheath, swung the bulky sack over his shoulder and set off once more.

But this time he did not head back to Cragaig. Instead he took a route further inland which would bring him out behind the village. He had in mind the deer's slot that he had seen earlier and suspected that the animal had been heading inland. Very often a deer moving in that direction in wild weather would take shelter in the cave which lay half a mile or so behind the village.

Since the wind was blowing straight inland, Alasdair walked a good way into the hills before cutting round towards the line of the village so that he should be well downwind of the animal. He walked fast, almost to the point of running, his stride never slowing. With the image of the woman close behind him. Now that he was on the move again and back into his own life he wanted to be rid of the woman. Yet her face with the teeth and the deep, steady eyes returned to him time and again. And the fall of her hair and the sprung softness of her breasts and all that was unknown.

At last Alasdair was parallel with the cave and he moved cautiously towards the rim of the ridge which separated him from the open valley above Cragaig. He crouched down and peered over the edge.

The shallow valley opened out below him. To the left it ended in the top of the slope above the village; to the right it climbed gradually up to the small heights which cut the headland off from the road. In front of him the flatness of the valley stretched a good six hundred yards before rising into a large hillside of heathers that climbed away into the flanks of Beinn Chreagach to the north.

In the valley the ground lay like a patchwork quilt. The clumps of rusty brackens alternated with the brown-white hill grasses, prune-coloured heathers, sudden excrescences of matt grey rocks and glades, strips and quarters of the endless peat-moss, speckled masses of wild-bright greens and browns and yellows. Away on the right, slightly up the valley, an outcrop of rock the size of a two-storey building poked harsh and grey from out of the brackens. At its base, as if a dirty thumb had pressed in the rock, a blackened hole. The cave.

Alasdair ran his eyes over the valley. At this time of the year the deer were perfectly camouflaged. The redness of their coats in the early autumn months had given away to the drab greyish-brown that made their shapes almost indistinguishable from the expanses of rock and grass. While they remained stationary they were invisible to all but the experienced eye of the hunter.

Now, with the winter wind running round the flank of the hill and battering at his eyes, Alasdair had difficulty in getting a clear view of the scene. His eyes came to rest on a dull shape a few yards below the cave. It had the vague outline of a deer feeding but through Alasdair's watering eyes it could well have been one of the myriad patches of darker colouring on the land. His eyes narrowed and his whole head strained forward as he concentrated, his breathing slowing to an imperceptible movement as he, quite suddenly the hunter, froze to the likeness of a rock.

For several minutes he crouched stock-still, conscious only of the distant spot with leg-like appendages that lay tucked into the midst of the jig-saw of the landscape. Up the valley on the back of the wind two hoodies came turning and tumbling, their ragged wing tips giving them the appearance of bits of flotsam carried inland on the turbulent air. They passed Alasdair and shrank slowly into the distance. The wind blew unchecked. Still Alasdair's eyes remained on that one spot, as if petrified in his head. Then, suddenly, the rims flickered and tightened. The spot had moved. Just the shifting of a leg and then stillness again but enough to confirm Alasdair's suspicions.

For another half-minute he waited, assuring himself that the animal had not seen him. Then he pulled himself backwards until he was below the skyline and turned away along the hillside. He moved quickly but without haste, working out his best route as he went. Across the hill, where the dead grasses, white and beige, bent and sprang beneath the hill winds, then southwards wide, moving round the far side of a small hill.

And eventually he came out far behind the cave, several hundred yards downwind of the deer. What he had seen had told him that the animal was a hind. A female of the species with her soft, unbelieving eyes. A tremor ran across his shoulders.

What exactly had happened to him on the shore was hard to say. But now he felt himself shaken out of his forty-five years, all the strands of his sensory system tautened, his flaccid mind spurred into new energies, so that he was dimly aware of the strength in his body and found unconscious pleasure in the driving of his legs and the elastic power of his back. This was the sudden and belated awakening of his man's self-awareness, the appreciation of himself as a male, which needed expression, needed demonstration before or with a female. He thought again of the woman of the eyes and mouth and recalled the way in which she had looked at him, a woman's look towards a man in which there was not only a seeking of contact in the mind but also appreciation of him, Alasdair Mór, in his bodily prowess.

Again, Alasdair's heart quickened at this memory and he swelled his lungs and breathed out deeply. And for all the disconcertment within him there was a strange look of excitement and pleasure on his face. It showed itself in a small enigmatic smile and a light, rhythmical contraction of his eyes as he walked stealthily into the wind in search of his prey. For all the slowness of his mind and the monotonous simplicity of his existence, Alasdair Mór possessed a soul of soft wax on which the infrequent dramas of his life pressed their long delicate fingers and left him with indelible memories. And thus marked, he walked onwards into the sea-wind.

At last he came up behind the outcrop of rock. Here he slipped the sack of firewood from his shoulders. Then he dropped to his hands and knees and crept forward through the heathers. Each yard he moved forward brought an extra expanse of the valley below into view and he froze for a few seconds until he was sure that the hind was not yet in sight. Onwards he moved until he was so close to the edge of the rock that the only ground still hidden was that immediately surrounding the cave below him. Unless the hind had already made off into the hills, she would be, as Alasdair had hoped, by the cave.

Finally he came to the brink and keeked over. Much to his delight he saw that the deer was standing with her head in the cave so that only the elegant shape of her body was in sight, a mere ten foot or so beneath him. He rolled away from the edge, tipped on to his side, unsheathed the great knife and stalked forward again.

Half rising to his feet he came up to the edge in a crouching position. The wind, streaming up the valley from off the sea, furrowed his face and blocked his hearing so that he stood poised in a thunderous silence. But the direction and very strength of the wind also ensured that the deer too heard nothing.

At the edge of the rock, Alasdair felt his body vibrating with excitement and anticipation. He raised his eyes for a second and saw the storm-flecked band of the sea, the running clouds, the grasses and brackens bent flat . . . he felt himself carrying the venting of all the elements. And he stood there in his hunter's crouch, knife in hand and with a glinting heart and the knowledge that he was strong and that the female lay beneath him. Several feet below, the hind was unaware of the impending danger. Alasdair took a quick look, judged the distance and dropped.

But as he went he dislodged a small stone and immediately the hind was on the alert. She raised her head and started to turn just as the great bulk of the man fell upon her.

Alasdair had counted on disabling the beast by breaking her back with the impact of his fall. She would have lain in paralysed pain and terror for only a few seconds while he had adjusted himself and slipped his knife into the jugular vein. But such were the reactions of the deer that in the second's warning she was already moving out of the cave when Alasdair struck her. She had half backed, half turned so that he landed on her shoulders where the strength of her forequarters were better equipped to withstand such a blow.

Down she went under the impact with Alasdair sitting high up on her, his left arm already round her throat. But she was a bigger beast than Alasdair had realised and after a moment of thrashing feet and bucking back she was up on her feet again and making off in blind terror across the valley with her grotesque burden slumped insecurely across her neck.

For the first yards Alasdair was in danger of losing his grip and falling off. There was no question of him attempting to use the knife for it was all he could do not to drop it as he used both arms to try and regain his balance.

His head was down on the neck of the hind so that he felt the coarse hair of the hide on his face. He smelt too those pungent, slightly acrid smells of the deer, a sensation which brought images of wildness and beauty, independence and para-doxical vulnerability. So that as his mount careered across the countryside, he found himself briefly forgetting his intentions of slaughter and instead, clutching the warm flesh, sucking in the deep smells, listening to the orgastic snortings and pantings of the panic-ridden animal, feeling the great life of the fiery creature beneath his body.

At one moment, as Alasdair pulled against the hind's neck in an attempt to bring himself squarely on to her back, the creature's head was twisted towards him and he caught sight of a dark eye, exophthalmic in a mixture of terror and excitement, gazing round at the weight of warmth and rich male smells that covered her.

THE DEAD OF WINTER

THE DEAD OF WINTER

The eyes of a female wide open. Was it terror or passion?

Along the northern edge of the valley the hind and her strange rider ran until Alasdair suddenly found himself in command. His knees gripped her flanks, his chest lay squarely on her back, his left arm held her tight about the join of neck and chest. With a flash of his right arm, the knife rose and fell into the hind's throat. For a moment nothing seemed to have happened. The hind ran on as if untouched. Then at one stride there was a slight falter, nothing more than an unevenness of rhythm and at the following stride the forelegs buckled. They were just carried through into the next stride and then the whole front half of the animal appeared to fold. Down she went at speed so that Alasdair was thrown forwards and deposited fiercely into the deep, rough grass.

But he was lucky in his fall and was no more than badly winded. By the time he had recovered and found his knife, the hind was half gone. She had tried to struggle to her feet and had gone down again. She had kicked and bounced in a pathetic attempt to escape, but now she lay twitching and turning on the ground. Alasdair came up to her from behind, saw the half-closed eye of despair and the bloody mess that disfigured the elegant line of her neck. Now he possessed her, controlled her beauty and he felt remorse.

'There there, now, dinne fret. We'll no be long.'
He spoke gently, leant over her and sliced
deftly across her neck. The blood ran, the creature
jerked and lay still. Alasdair Mór's passion had
run its course.

The hind was soon gralloched and decapitated,
Alasdair's knowledgeable fingers feeling out the
neck joints and locating the point where a sharp
twist would sever the bone structure leaving
him only some simple knife work to remove the
head. With the lightened carcass on his shoulders,
Alasdair walked slowly back to the village.

He had time to joint the hind, hang the sections in the outhouse and then return to the cave
for the sack of firewood before the light began to
fail.

That night he fell into a deep, dreamless sleep.

7

As they passed over the ridge of the swell the bows dropped like a see-saw unbalanced and the boat slid with sickening speed towards the oily trough beyond. Moving away from the stern the immense bulk of the passing wave rolled quickly onwards up the coast, its back rounded with liquid muscle, its height exaggerated seen from behind so that it blotted out half the cliff.

A glance over his shoulder gave Alasdair a flashing picture of a new mass of water which was bearing down on him. In the second that he turned, the following swell seemed to be puffing itself up like a blackcock in display, threatening to swamp the boat by its sheer mass. The water of the trough and of the hind slopes of the last wave were marbled with streakings of foam.

Again the tip of the boat was suddenly halted and then lifted by an upsurging force. It tilted the boat fiercely so that Alasdair had to brace himself against the boards and then as the main body of water came beneath him he felt himself pushed vertically upwards until the whole expanse of the rolling sea came into sight. He looked down along the emptiness of vast ridges and valleys of polished dark greens and greys; he saw large slicks of creaminess, seemingly anchored, riding the backs of the swell; gulls and kittiwakes twisting and turning and foraging beneath the very feet of vast banks of water; the unswerving mission of a skart heading out to sea scraping over the heaving waters. And then, just as he felt the boat being carried backwards by the kick of the swell, he was over the top and falling, falling again.

There would be time for two or three powerful strokes of the oars before the next wave was beneath him. He pulled hard and the boat streamed down the bank and across the deceptive calm of the valley before it was once more braked by the arching shoulders of the swell.

Progress was slow. Under the late afternoon light of a sullen sky Alasdair Mór was taking his boat out into the face of the seas that rolled in from the southwest. He wanted to head due south, down the coast to Port nam Freumh, but the swell was too great for the size of his boat and so he headed farther west, planning to swing round later and come into the harbour with the swell running behind him. Slow as it was, he was safe enough while he kept the boat head on to the seas.

For ten minutes or so he moved down the coast. At one point, as he hung on the crest of a wave, he caught sight of a long angular fin lying in a trough some distance away to the seaward side of him. The next time he rose he turned quickly and saw it again. It disappeared sleekly into a large sea and Alasdair just had time to see the whip of a powerful tail as it pushed forward into the water.

'The bastard!' Alasdair was glad that the shape of his boat lay disguised in the shifting hills of the swell for what he had seen was a thresher, one of the Atlantic sharks. Compared with the killer whale which occasionally appeared on that coast and which seemed to kill viciously, simply for pleasure, the thresher was a docile enough creature. But it was inquisitive and often nosed round small boats, sometimes rising up beneath them and capsizing them. All the fishermen feared them, with reason, and Alasdair was glad that in a few minutes he would be doubling back and running with the seas to the harbour.

In spite of the chill in the air he felt the sweat prickling on his shoulders as he struggled with the boat. As he ran up on a wave he paused to adjust his cap and squeezed a salt hand over the stubble of his screwed-up face. He would be thankful to be home. This time of year was bad, for the weather had not yet settled into the wind and rains of the full winter and he was still trying to put in a bit of fishing. But he had to spend long hours at sea for all that he got and in many ways he looked forward to the day when he could beach his boat and just wait for the spring.

At last he came to a point where he could turn and head for the shore. In the few seconds between the passing of one wave and the arrival of the next he had got the boat round and into line with the swell. And now he rose and fell in a different pattern, speeding out of control with the momentum of the waves and then slipping back into a state of temporary calm.

And then, in the space of four waves, it happened. First, he saw a boat, out to the south of Maisgeir. The next time he rose he saw the dim shape of a man using one of the oars, still on the thole-pin, to beat at the surface of the sea. There was something desperate in his actions and Alasdair knew immediately what it was. And then he caught a glimpse of the glossy back and ugly fin of the thresher rise briefly by the boat and the boat jump and lift, casting the man helplessly into the sea. Again Alasdair fell and the scene disappeared.

'By Christ!' And as Alasdair sank beneath the level of the swell he was already turning his boat. Round it came and straight away he was bending his back into the oars so that the boat virtually took off as it breasted the wave. There was no conscious decision, no consideration of the danger involved in finding himself out in such seas in the darkness. There was simply the knowledge that there was a man in the water and that he must be found quickly, at all costs.

As he rowed, Alasdair took in all the details of the situation. By the time he got to the capsized boat the darkness would be upon them and there would be little sense in trying to get back to the harbour in such conditions. But if he could pick the man up and get in behind Maisgeir it might be possible to make a landing on the skerry in the more sheltered waters. Once there they would have to sit out the night and hope that daylight would bring them no worse seas. But all this would come later. First there was the man to be found.

Deep inside, Alasdair knew that the man must be An Sionnach. There was no other person working this part of the coast and old Angus McKechnie who lived with his wife and two girls a few miles to the north never worked this far south, let alone in weather such as this. And so he was out to help An Sionnach. In many ways it was strange that he should be doing this for the man was his open enemy and, in addition, he had no sympathy for any man who could knock a woman into the sea and leave her to drown. The woman. It would have been only too easy to turn a blind eye and go home, leaving the wretched man spluttering and choking in the heavy seas until exhaustion slowly relaxed his grip on the cold, slippery bottom of the boat. He would have vanished without trace and there was nobody about who could have witnessed Alasdair's failure to help. And yet among the men of the sea, emergencies like this came before personal feelings. You could save a man from drowning and a day later beat the hell out of him over some private feud.

THE DEAD OF WINTER

Foreigners from the south always found it strange that the men who spent their lives working the seas could not swim. To them it seemed one of the obvious forms of insurance against a miserable death; but they knew little of the ways of the sea, had little concept of the powers that the Atlantic held over the men with its combination of thundering waves and icy waters. The fishermen would never talk seriously about this, as if out of superstition, but said that if they had to die they would rather die quickly. The inference was that if there were seas large enough to sink a boat then there would be little chance for a fully clothed man whether he swam or not.

It took Alasdair Mór near on twenty minutes to reach the capsized boat. In the half-light he caught no sight of it until he was only a few boat-lengths away. Then at last he saw the dark shape of the upturned hull wallowing in the silent grey mountains of the sea. Slumped across it, an irregular form like the baggage on a pack horse.

Alasdair closed the distance to about ten yards and then, holding the boat as steady as possible, turned and shouted.

'Sionnach! Can ye hear me? Are ye there?'

'Aye.' The answer came like a groan. The waves bucked and slid; the sounds were only of the water against the boats.

'Here, I'm coming for ye. Can ye take a hold of my boat and I'll try and get ye in.'

'Aye.'

Alasdair manœuvred cautiously, trying to bring the boats as close as possible without crushing the man between them. When he was only a few feet away Alasdair shipped an oar and held still with the other. The bulk across the capsized boat stirred and began to turn. The man looked round, tried to gauge the distance and swung a feeble arm towards Alasdair's gunwale. But at that moment a mountainous swell lifted both boats apart and broke An Sionnach's hold on his own wreck. With a pathetic slither and a mumbled curse that was blocked by a faceful of brine he slid down between the two boats and vanished.

Alasdair fell forward, abandoning control of his boat, and hung over the side. The chill wind of the November night flickered across the arcing backs of the sea. The swell rose and fell in dour silence, its flanks like matt metal bending and forming changelessly. The thick tweeding of the clouds stretched overhead with no more than a weak shimmer of light.

Water slapped against the boat, breaking into a scattering of spray over Alasdair's arms and face but he scarcely blinked as his wax-parchment face peered out on the gloom. His eyes were shrivelled, glistening beads in the shadows of their sockets, as he scanned the sea for a sign of An Sionnach. For some seconds there was nothing. Nothing but the bleak infinities of a night sea and sky. Then, only a few yards away, a beating arm broke the surface and was followed by a raucous choking sound as An Sionnach's head came clear of the depths. A fearsome spouting and gurgling as he rid himself of sea water and gasped in fresh air.

In a flash Alasdair was at the oars and over to the drowning man. By the time he got there An Sionnach had gone under again but Alasdair grasped what still showed of him and heaved him back to the surface. And he pulled with all his strength until An Sionnach's shoulders were over the gunwale. An Sionnach seemed to be in his death throes for the sounds which came from him were those of a beast being throttled.

The two men hung there, embracing over the gunwale, as An Sionnach fought to regain his breath. Suddenly with an involuntary contraction An Sionnach gagged violently and spewed a mixture of sea water and vomit into Alasdair's face and then slumped with a groan. Alasdair shook his head in revulsion.

'Sionnach! for Christ's sake take hold of yourself man. The sea'll put us down if ye canne get into the boat. Come in with ye.' And he pulled at the sodden mass once more. At this first attempt the boat heeled over dangerously and threatened to go under as the sea poured in.

'For Christ's sake, man, come on! Now!' And as the next wave slipped up under the boat both men gave a wild heave and the body fell head first into the bottom of the boat. Alasdair clambered across the slumped figure and took hold of

the oars, furiously seeking to turn the boat into
the swell before the next wave swamped them.
With the two men aboard and a quantity of
water lying in the bilges the boat lay relatively
low in the sea and was at the mercy of the waves.

An Sionnach stirred and dragged himself out
of the bilge water. He sat heavily on the stern
bench.

'Can ye find the wee bucket in the stern? Ye'll
need to lose us some of yon water.' An Sionnach
seemed to understand for he turned and foraged
in the dark until, with a metal clank, his hand
found the bucket. He started to bail desultorily.

Meanwhile Alasdair had turned the boat and
was running with the swell in the direction of
Maisgeir. But it was difficult to make out anything in the darkness beyond a dozen yards and
as they moved he kept his ears open for the tell-
tale sound of surf. At last it came, out on the port
bow and Alasdair turned to see the dim lump of
the skerry.

Approaching it from the south Alasdair knew
that it would be safe to pass close to the
rocks for the water was deep at this end. But in
the darkness the distance was deceptive and
it was a few minutes before they drew level with
the skerry. For anyone who did not know the
waters as well as Alasdair did, the approach might
have been disconcerting. On the side open to the
Atlantic the swell rolled in silently enough but
when it came up against the rocks of Maisgeir

131

it exploded with a dull boom, the spray flying high and hissing across the breadth of the small island.

They passed close by, leaving the surf to port and continuing onwards as if they intended to head straight for the coast. However, as soon as they were past the tip of Maisgeir Alasdair swung the boat in behind the block of rocks. With comparatively little wind and a straightforward ground swell running, the sheltered waters behind Maisgeir were strangely calm. With a final lifting of the stern in the passing swell, the boat slipped into smooth water.

There was no place on Maisgeir where a boat could be drawn up from the sea and to leave it moored to the rocks would be to leave it to a night's chafing and banging, even in the relative calmness of these waters. But there was little choice and they would have to make the best of it. So Alasdair brought the boat in close until they came up against the steep rocks. He held the boat off with one hand and turned to An Sionnach.

'Get ye ashore now. We'll be best here till the light.'

An Sionnach grunted an assent and came squelching up the boat towards Alasdair. He passed him and Alasdair caught the smell of salt and wet wool. A moment later An Sionnach was ashore and holding the boat. Alasdair went to the stern and after digging around came back

with a large hank of rope. This he attached to the
port thole-pin so that it dangled down the side of
the boat as a makeshift buffer. Then he threw a
line from the stern to An Sionnach and, seizing
another from the bows, slipped ashore himself.

They made the boat fast to the rocks and looked
around for a place to spend the night. Even on
the landward side of the small island they found
themselves open to the swarms of spray which
rose up from the other side as the seas broke
on the rocks. But eventually they stumbled across
a spot where a smooth slab of rock, only a few feet
above the high water mark, was protected from
the spray by a rough outcrop. Here they settled
themselves down as best they could, wedged together, partly from a lack of space, partly to
conserve what little warmth they had left in them.
There would be about eleven hours until first light.

An Sionnach was trembling with cold but there
was little that Alasdair could do for him. For a
long while they just sat there without moving,
listening to the thumping of the surf behind them
and waiting for the sheets of spray to pass overhead and land like a hail of shot on the water
beyond. A few yards to their left the boat ground
and banged harshly against the rock. Out to
their right vague shapes swept past in the dark.

Alasdair raised his hand to scratch his face and
felt something cold and glutinous on his cheek.
He remembered and went down to the water to
wash himself. As he came back he saw through an

opening in the rocks that far out over the sea the clouds were beginning to break up and a thin glow of moonlight was shining.

'The moon's up. We might be getting a wee bit of light later the night.'

'Good on it.' An Sionnach's reply was dead, sullen.

This, then, was the passing of the storm. Three days earlier it had leapt up overnight, lashing the sea into a turmoil, driving and backhanding the coast with volleys of tremendous power so that it was all that Alasdair could do to keep himself on his feet as he stood on the cliffs at Cragaig the following morning. For two days and nights it had gone on, bringing hours of torrential rain that had cut visibility down to a minimum. Alasdair had huddled gloomily in his house, whittling away at a piece of wood in an attempt to while away the hours.

And then, suddenly, that morning, the wind and rain had passed on, leaving behind leaden skies and a heavy ground swell. This was the normal aftermath of these vicious Atlantic storms but it usually played itself out within a day or two. With a bit of luck, Alasdair now thought to himself, the seas would be down by the morning.

'Yon swell'll be down by the morrow, I'm thinking.'

'Aye, could be, right enough.' Alasdair sat down again and wedged himself back beside An Sionnach.

Was this really the man who had vowed enmity towards him? The man who had struck the woman into the sea? Alasdair felt the man beside him, quiet, inoffensive, a good deal smaller than himself. He could see nothing of him except the dim shape of his feet. Boots full of water.

'Ye'd best move yourself about a bit if ye dinne want to catch your death of cold.' Alasdair spoke factually, without a trace of feeling.

'Yer fucking erse! Ye'll no have the satisfaction of seeing me die. I've a good while to go yet, mind ye, and I'll no be told what to do by the like of ye.' An Sionnach's answer came like a wildcat's claws, slashing out in warning. Alasdair could not follow this man. He had meant nothing beyond a practical suggestion and the man had turned on him. He felt An Sionnach's eyes on him through the darkness. A heavy silence settled itself between the two men and without more ado they prepared themselves to sit out the night.

For a couple of hours they remained there wide awake, frozen to the marrow, eyes looking out on to the depths of nothingness. Every now and again one of them would shift slightly, trying to relieve his cramped body or there would be a snuffle or cough as the damp night air penetrated their lungs. And then, gradually, as the night moved on with its unchanging features of sound and sightlessness, a damp-eyed sleep, more a numbing lethargy, began to creep over the consciousness of the two men. Such was their discomfort that when they first felt the soft, hirsute hand of sleep run lightly over their senses, they blinked in disbelief. But it returned again and again, brought on by the exhaustion of the seas, and with little jerks and nods they both, in turn, fell into a light sleep.

Sometimes Alasdair woke to hear his companion breathing thickly in his sleep; sometimes he woke to feel An Sionnach watching him, breathing stilled, eyes alert. Once or twice An Sionnach got to his feet and stamped around the ledge trying to revive his circulation and Alasdair as he slept and woke lost track of the dimensions of time, sometimes feeling that An Sionnach had been on his feet for hours and other times that he had sat down as soon as he had stood up.

Once, late in the night, he woke to find the moon high in the sky behind them, shining out on to the sea towards the coast. The swell, already considerably smaller, rolled past in noiseless state, the waters thick and evil in the cold light. The lower half of An Sionnach's sleeping form showed clearly in the moonlight, but the rest of him still lay deep unseen, buried in the dank shadows.

Alasdair watched the seas for what seemed like an age and then once again, lulled by their monotonous movement, he fell asleep. He fell into the deep, pre-dawn sleep of exhaustion and dreamed a long, complicated dream of chaos and unreality.

THE DEAD OF WINTER

He was woken by the bugle-like cries of a large flock of herring gulls, hovering low and diving at a shoal of fish just below the surface a dozen yards to the south of the skerry. Alasdair blinked and shook his head. The sun was not yet up but the sky, cleared of clouds, was light with the thin gleam of white to the east. Alasdair's brain was slow in unravelling but it was not long in realising that he was alone on the shelf of rock.

'Where's yon bugger got to the now?' Almost out of instinct he glanced the other way towards the boat. Or, at least, to where the boat had been for now there was nothing but the rock and seaweed exposed by the low tide.

'Ye bloody bastard, Sionnach!' Alasdair's small vocabulary was strengthened by the vigour with which he mouthed his disgust and fury. 'Yon's a bad bugger.' To steal a man's boat was one thing, but to steal it from the man who had saved your life only hours before was hard to forgive. Alasdair scanned the sea towards the coast and found nothing. He clambered to the top of the skerry and looked all around but again saw nothing.

Alasdair was not too concerned by being stranded on the skerry because the sky and sea gave every indication of still, peaceful weather. It would only be a matter of time before a fishing boat passed and with luck he would be able to attract their attention.

He rubbed his hands together and slapped at his body for he was deadly cold on this raw

November morning after a chilling night at sea. But he scarcely thought of this as he wandered around the tidal rocks of the skerry. Once again he found himself turning over in his mind the callousness, the viciousness of the man who had just made off with his boat. Once his initial anger had died down, Alasdair was more eaten up with curiosity about An Sionnach's actions than by any thoughts of revenge. Though there were moments when he regretted having saved the man.

Alasdair Mór saw every detail of that day's life. He watched the sun hoist itself up from behind the hills, first sending its fingers of brightness slipping through the valleys and high passes and then, as the whole face of the patriarch came clear of the skyline, galvanising the grey flapping of the sea into the life of the full day. But long before this had happened the skerry had burst into action. Gulls of every description plundered the surrounding waters and rampaged about the tidal rocks on the look-out for the crabs which scuttled backwards and forwards among the weeds. On the open side of the skerry gannets soared and dropped like darts from great heights to come up beneath some unsuspecting fish. The air was full of the ploshing sounds as the hunters struck deep.

The tide rose and fell with the sun and still Alasdair was marooned. Twice fishing boats passed but they were too far out to sea for his shouts and gesticulations to be of any avail. After each failure he sank into a state of apathy and sat brooding on the highest point, staring out towards the horizon. And as the light began to fail he realised sourly that he was to have another night in the open.

By now he had had nothing to eat for near on thirty-six hours and his stomach was beginning to twist and whine. He slipped down to the tidal area and by means of a heavy rock succeeded in knocking loose a quantity of limpets. These he carried back to his perch and consumed greedily, digging out the rubbery animals with the point of his knife. There was little to them beyond a strong salty taste but it was enough to pacify his stomach and he finished by feeling better able to face the tedium and cold of the coming night.

That second night on Maisgeir Alasdair slept little. The hours of exposure had sent a deep chill seeping into his bones which the tepidness of the midday sun had done little to remedy. If he slept at all it was more from boredom than tiredness. On and on the sea lapped at the rocks and on and on Alasdair sat staring out into the darkness, with his knees drawn up and his hands tucked beneath his jerkin and sweater.

And that night when Alasdair was alone and the moon was hidden by clouds, he might well have been hundreds of miles out in the ocean for all that he could see or hear. There was no fear in him as he kept his vigil, only a chilled numbness of mind and body and a sullen desire for survival.

As soon as there was enough light to see his hands in front of him he was up and creeping about, endlessly pausing and turning an ear to listen for the sound of a boat. And sure enough, as the half-light came, he caught the far-off thumping of an engine. As he waited for it to get nearer he tried to estimate its course and was eventually overjoyed to see his hopes fulfilled and a snub-nosed form appearing only a hundred yards or so west of the skerry.

The boat came creeping down from the north, ploughing sluggishly through the dawn sea. Although he knew his shouts would be inaudible above the noise of the engine he was unable to restrain himself and bellowed madly as he waved his arms. There was, indeed, a man on deck who appeared to be mending one of the stays but it was sheer luck that he happened to look up at that moment and see the unlikely sight of a man standing in the early morning light on the top of a small skerry. In fact he seemed, at first, not to trust his sight for it was a while before he moved. But then he walked quickly to the wheelhouse and put his head through the door. A few seconds later the engine slowed and the boat turned towards the rocks. Ten minutes later Alasdair was aboard and gulping down tea and a piece. And a dram or two.

Alasdair did not know the fishermen for they were from way south on the mainland so he told

them a story about being wrecked on Maisgeir.
The fishermen offered to put him down at an old
disused pier three-quarters of an hour further
south. Alasdair accepted and fell asleep.

And so it was that a short while later he found
himself back on dry land. The boat's engine
roared and they were on their way. Alasdair
turned back along the path to pick up the road
northwards towards Cragaig.

8

AULAY closed the door of his house at Achateny
and took a deep breath of still, fresh air. To his
left the steadings and the main house sprawled
untidily, a great quagmire of mud filling most of
the foreground where a small group of cattle
stood gazing hopelessly at him. All about, the hillsides lay camped, glistening here and there as the
acres of wetness were caught by an edge of the sun.

'Yon woman!' Aulay had escaped from a sullen
Martha who had been trying to shame him with
his endless bouts of drinking. Two nights before
he had come home from the town somewhat the
worse for the drink and had stumbled into the
kitchen humming glowingly to himself. Coming
unsteadily down the small flight of stairs he had
reached for support and had brought down a
whole shelf of crockery with terrible results. The
noise had woken Martha who had shouted down
to him from the bedroom and as he turned
guiltily towards the cry he had trodden in the
cat's bowl of food, lost his balance and fallen,
bringing down with him a large saucepan con-
taining the next day's soup. He had lain there on
the cold stone floor, slightly dazed with the mess
of soup splattered across him like vomit and

surrounded by a landscape of broken china. Martha had come hurriedly downstairs and had been too frightened by the sight to remember to be angry. The next day Aulay had made himself scarce and it was only now, thirty-six hours later, that he had caught the inevitable lash of his wife's tongue.

Beneath the whisky's watery film his blue eyes sparkled with the childlike pleasure of rebellion and, smacking his hands together, he set off with his two dogs towards the road in the direction of the Cragaig road-end and the town. But as he came out on the road he happened to glance back along it and noticed a distant figure coming towards him. He paused and screwed up his tough old face trying to make out who it might be. And odd as it seemed, there was no mistaking the shambling gait, the improbable pigeon-toed stepping and the dangling arms.

'And what the hell will Alasdair Mór be doing coming from thataway at this hour?' And because he was inquisitive and because he was friendly but mostly because he was never in a hurry to get to work, he sat himself down on a rock to wait for Alasdair. Slowly but surely the shape grew nearer.

'Hello there, Alasdair. And how are ye the day?'

'Hello Aulay. Och and I could be worse. And how are ye keeping yourself?'

'Oh well, I'm no complaining. . . . And what are ye away from down there?' And so, slowly, the story came out. Alasdair was no great storyteller and it needed all Aulay's prompting to fill in the details. When Alasdair came to a halt and stood there with his arms swinging and not knowing what to say next—for he had not yet decided what he was going to do—Aulay, opening cautiously, added his bit of the story.

'Yon's hell of a queer . . . and what's more I'm thinking you might want to know that yesterday afternoon when I was out on the hill, An Sionnach's woman was up to the house to ask Martha if she'd seen the man for the woman had no set eyes on him since the day before. And ye know the queerest thing, Martha said that the woman was no worried at all. An Sionnach's boat was away and the woman had no seen him in all that while . . . you'd think the lass might have been afeared for her man, but no, not a bit of it, not at all. And when Martha said they must be on to the coastguard rightaway yon woman got in a hell of a fret and begged her to do no such thing. It's a right queer business altogether. . . . Did ye see which way the bugger took your boat from Maisgeir?'

'No—I never saw a sign of the bugger.' A pause as the two men looked at each other. It came to them both that somehow the man had got himself drowned. 'But the sea was no so bad yesterday.' Alasdair's comment was the logical continuation of their thoughts.

'No, it was calm enough. . . . And what are ye thinking on doing the now, Alasdair?'

'Well, I'd best be away home to look to the cow.

But I think I'll be over to An Sionnach's house to see if the bastard's turned up. I've a few things to say to yon man.'

'Aye, ye will that, I'm sure.'

'Right ye are, Aulay, I'd best away.' And without waiting for Aulay to reply Alasdair turned on his heel and started up the road.

'Will I see ye tomorrow at the road-end?' Aulay's shout carried clearly in the still air.

'Aye.' Alasdair never turned nor even slowed, but his answer plumed from his mouth, peeled high over him and came back to Aulay before the older man called to his dogs and set off at a tangent to the nearby hillside.

Alasdair stamped up the road for the mile or so to the Cragaig turning and then branched off up the indistinct path and was soon lost to sight in the expanse of mottled countryside.

Physically he was tired after his two nights on the skerry, but he pushed his body onwards, his mind alert with undercurrents of anxiety over the boat. When he arrived back at Cragaig the relief and security he felt did much to soothe his mind and he set to the animals with the affection which can only spring from separation. He chaffed them and indulged them and would have been quite happy to stay at home for the rest of the day if it had not been for the nagging worries of uncertainty about the boat. There would be no more gentle speaking to An Sionnach. He would get himself over to the house and make the man sorry for what he had done. And get him to hand over the boat and then there would be an end to it.

He tidied up and made himself something to eat and still chewing on the last piece, he slammed the door behind him and walked down the slope towards the burn.

He took the path along the cliffs rather than cutting over the hills and soon the village was left far behind.

The day had remained still and clear with only scattered clutches of clouds spotting the sky. The sea below looked dormant beneath its surface film of many-sided sheen. The coast too was surprisingly quiet with only the occasional gull on the move. The Achateny sheep had moved their grazing elsewhere.

As he walked he kept his eyes on the shore for any sign of the boat. Quite suddenly he realised that he was standing where he had stood a week or two before and saw again in his mind's eye the couple on the rocks. An Sionnach. And the woman. The woman with her eyes and teeth, her strong body and her boldness. Had all that happened? To him, Alasdair Mór? He paused briefly and then moved on. As he walked he was deep in thought. Absent-mindedly he picked his nose, burrowing like a ferret into his nostrils. He wondered if the woman would be with An Sion-nach. In many ways he hoped that she would not be there for it would make it harder for him to speak openly to the man. Why had she acted

so strangely when Martha had wanted to call
out the coastguard? Ach, there was no telling
with yon pair. But it was queer, right enough.

At last he rounded the angle of the cliff and
saw away along the hillside the squat form of An
Sionnach's croft. Smoke coiled from the single
chimney, a plait of milky-tea vapour. So they
were at home. Well, by Christ, they were going
to have a visitor whether they liked it or not.
Alasdair breathed deeply and hastened his pace.

The croft lay by itself on an open hillside, bare
to the prevailing winds with neither tree nor
companionable hillock to bring any feeling of
warmth and homeliness to the place. About it,
various piles of rubble, the only visible remains of
a couple of other houses which had stood there in
Alasdair's grandfather's time. And, in summer,
even these remnants were overrun by copses of
rank nettles. The rusty form of an ancient
ploughshare lay disguised by the bracken. At
the back of the house, where the hillside came down
to it, there was the look of coldness, moss and
slime and all the other attributes of dampness.
The whole homestead reeked of neglect.

Alasdair suddenly felt his intentions waver. His
natural shyness momentarily laid a hand on his
heart and he no longer knew what he was going
to say. There was a great difference between
finding oneself thrown into a quarrel and going
into someone else's house to get angry in cold
blood. And so part of this slow-moving man of

the country jibbed at the coming trial, but then he remembered the treachery of An Sionnach and the loss of his boat and again there arose in him the silent chokings of anger. He stepped forward once more and made his way over to the house.

He came up to the door and banged twice with the side of his fist. No sound, no sign of life came from the house. Now he stood there feeling foolish, feeling that his plans had fallen flat. But he banged again just to make sure and this time there was a slight sound of a chair scraping backwards and a second or two later the door opened a few inches. Through the gap, wearing a grey apron over her blue dress, the woman.

'Oh . . . good day to ye . . . I hope I'm no disturbing ye. . . .' Alasdair begins to lose hold of his plans, stammering out politenesses as he seeks to regain his balance. The woman stands stock still, eyes steadily on the face of the man who bobs around nervously, casting his gaze everywhere but at her. Never a flicker of response on her face.

'Is he home?'

'No. No just now.' The smooth mount of the woman's mouth parts, showing her bands of teeth and the words come forth gently in the breathy song of the Outer Isles speech. Her eyelids flitter slightly in a momentary acknowledgement of recognition. Alasdair notices her hand on the door, long fingered but reddened by work. She sees him stare and shyly lowers her hand.

'Oh, I see. And would ye be expecting him back the now?'

'Well, it could be. Was it something important ye had to see him about?'

'Aye, well I think he has my boat and I'll be needing it back.' Alasdair's understatement avoids involving the woman in the harsher truth of the story. He feels the need to shield her from the treachery of her man. Yet he still needs to see An Sionnach. 'Well, thank ye anyway. I think I'll be best to wait on him a while.' And he moves off a few yards, but she, ever so quietly and in a nervous, tentative voice: 'Will ye no come away in? Ye'd be more comfortable.'

'Aye, well that'd be grand.' And he lowers his eyes and comes shuffling back to enter the house.

For all its drab exterior the inside of the croft has another, more warming, feel to it. Basically the room is the same as Alasdair's, the same as most of the crofts on that coast, but here one notices the hand of a woman. The shelves where the pots and pans are kept are scrubbed clean and covered with neat strips of newspaper. The hearth, where a small fire burns, has recently been brushed clean of ashes and excessive soot. The window ledges, which in Alasdair's house are full of little oddments, are here dusted and the few things that lie on them are tidily arranged. A large blanket box over in the far corner stands with its lid open, revealing clean clothes. Two paraffin lamps, brightly polished, stand on the small farmhouse table near the fire. All about, the stone floor has been swept and scrubbed. Alasdair marvels at it all.

'Will ye take a cup of tea? I was just after making myself some.'

'Aye, I will that.' And Alasdair sits down and leans back on the wooden chair, with his face taut and his mouth in a grin, as the woman goes about the business of making tea. He sees her bend to fill the kettle from a small barrel of water, sees the long curve of her back and the weight of her breasts, wonders at the neat economy of her movements. He notices the unsmiling features of her face and the steadiness of her eyes and knows that she is thinking but cannot guess of what. The kettle is placed over the fire, the cups and saucers and spoons laid out; the milk is poured into the cups; the teapot is readied. All this without pause, a ceaseless chain of unhurried actions that keeps the woman from having to stand still beneath Alasdair's gaze. Eventually, everything is prepared but still the kettle needs to boil. She earns herself another few moments' grace by wiping over the already clean table but then is at a loss as to what to do. Her fingers entwine, she looks about, gazes through the window and then turns back.

'No so bad the day.'

'Right enough, it's no so bad.' Alasdair continues to consider her and then says: 'Was he away early this morning?'

'Well. . . .' A long pause during which she fiddles with her apron. Then: 'Aye, early enough' and she casts a nervous glance in his direction. Somehow she knows that he sees the lie.

'He'll have things to do, I'm sure.'

'Oh, aye.' Another tense silence.

'Ye took a nasty fall yon day on the shore.' Alasdair's boldness surprises him. But just then the kettle starts to boil.

'Ach good, the kettle's boiled at last. Do ye take sugar?'

'Aye, thank ye, two.' And his boldness is blocked.

He looks down at his lap as if aware that he has overstepped the mark. He scratches the back of his head, touches his cap and in one movement sweeps if off and on to his knees.

'Here ye are then.' And the woman comes across to him with his cup, keeping her eyes on it as if to make sure that it does not spill. Alasdair hears the flustering of her skirt and watches her moving towards him. A wisp of her dark hair has fallen loose from her bun and hangs, springlike, over the down by her ear.

He takes the cup and saucer from her and almost before he has time to realise her nearness, she has turned and gone back to the fire where she sits down on a small stool and starts to drink her tea. But in the second that she was near him Alasdair's keen senses have caught the smell of the woman, the warmth of floury skin, the covering of peat smoke and the tinge of green-apple sourness.

Not a word passes between them as they drink and both keep their eyes to the ground. Occasionally the peats hiss or a sheep bleats, out behind the house. The smell of the fire covers everything.

Alasdair gulps down the last mouthful and deposits the cup noisily on the table. The woman still keeps her attention on her tea. Now Alasdair is staring at her again with that old thinking face of his so that he looks amused, quizzical.

'D'ye like it here then?'

'Aye, it's nice enough.'

'Aye, it's grand . . . but it's a lonely life for a woman. Are ye in to the village now and then?'

'No, he has to go in himself often enough so I just ask him to bring what I need.'

'Oh aye.' They have been looking at each other during these last words and now, though a silence falls once more between them, they continue to stare, Alasdair open-faced like a small child, she, An Sionnach's woman, more composed, but with a look of despair on her face. They remain like this for perhaps five seconds and then she drops her eyes, stands up and walks across to the window. She looks out, searching, finds nothing, but stays standing there.

'No sign of himself yet?' The woman does not find words to reply and shakes her head. 'Well, I'd best on my way then.' And he gets up, puts on his cap and thanking her for the tea, makes for the door. As he opens it the woman calls to him.

'Alasdair!' He pauses and turns and she is trying to find words to say something. She looks down and says quietly: 'Mind how ye go.'

Alasdair looks puzzled and then replies; 'Aye, I will that. Cheerio.'

'Cheerio.' And he is gone.

He walked away from the house, heading south. Out over the smooth grass by the house and into the heathers. The sun keeked down on the small corner of the land from behind a bank of clouds. He made out for the cliffs again, intent on scouring the coast for any sign of An Sionnach or the boat. At one moment he looked back to the house. Nothing but the thin twine of smoke.

What had the woman meant? What sort of cryptic message was there in her parting words? Or had there been no message, just a friendly way of talking? No, it seemed to Alasdair that she had been wanting to tell him something. Something of An Sionnach's intentions perhaps? And why had she lied to him about An Sionnach when everything pointed so clearly to him having vanished? Oh how he longed for his boat back and the return to his peaceful winter life!

But, as always, Alasdair Mór settled the worries in his mind by turning to the job in hand. He went along the cliff-top, following its wriggles and indentations mile upon mile, keeking over the edge with his mad eyes ranging into every corner of the coast in search of the boat. For a long while he saw nothing but the ragged shore, the

black pilings of boulders and wrack where the
coast lay beaten and shredded by the seas; but
then, way down below him, there showed the
dark form of a boat. It lay with its prow on a
scrap of black sand, wedged in between two
fortlike rocks, with the rising tide creeping up
round its stern. Alasdair's face set in grim
triumph.

He found a way down the cliff, following the
twists and tumblings of a burn still full from
the storm, until he came out on the level of the
sea. Here there were no raised beaches and the
slope of the cliff vanished into the sea with only
the dark jumble of rocks underlining the division.
But the rocks of the shore were mammoth
boulders, many standing higher than Alasdair's
head, with skirts and hangings of bitter-coloured
tangle and their lower sides encrusted with
barnacles and limpets and clusters of coaly blue
mussels. In among the wilderness of these rocks
the man slipped, poking his way through dark
cavernous openings, across glassy pools where
minute crabs and sea snails wandered among the
pinks and purples and greens of anemones and
algae, over banks of thick tangle which squeaked
and popped under his weight. This tidal world
was sealed by the expansive smells of low water:
the salt, the iodine, the jelly fish, the crustaceans.

Through this he wandered like a hunting beast,
his nostrils spreading and closing at the homely
smells, snuffling, drawing, blowing, his head

hung lower as he stooped with shining eyes towards the shore life. For a while he almost forgot about the boat and stopped to pick up shells and odd growths, finding himself side-tracked by the renewed novelty of each and every corner.

But then, over the top of a smaller rock, he saw the bows of the boat, knew it to be his own, and dropping the dog whelk which he had been examining, made his way quickly through the last complexities of the rocks.

Not only was the boat his but it also appeared to be intact, with the oars neatly shipped and the bow line well secured by a heavy boulder—just as if An Sionnach had carefully moored the boat for his future use. Alasdair turned and looked about, half expecting to see the man watching him. But then he remembered that An Sionnach must have come ashore early the previous morning and was probably far away now, thinking it best to keep out of sight for a while. Had An Sionnach gone first to tell his woman? Perhaps . . . that would explain some of her evasiveness. Well, to hell with the man! He was not going to waste his time chasing An Sionnach round the country-side. And perhaps now An Sionnach felt himself vindicated, having twice made a fool of him. As far as he was concerned he would prefer to forget the whole matter so long as An Sionnach kept out of his way in the future.

Since it was still early in the afternoon and the

weather showed no sign of turning, Alasdair decided to take the boat straight back to Port nam Freumh. Two or three hours later as the dusk came down, he stepped ashore at the harbour and made his way up the cliffs to Cragaig to take up his lonely life where he had left it two days before.

Once back in the village he dealt summarily with the animals and retired to the house. As the door closed behind him, the outside world with its threats and problems was snuffed out. All the past happenings with An Sionnach shrank to mere sketches. Though the memory of the woman—as such memories often do with solitary men—remained like a glowing night-light in the corner of his mind.

That evening, in compensation for the hardships, Alasdair took good care of himself. First of all, he got a good fire going, enjoying a sudden bout of carefree extravagance with his winter peats. When this was giving out a good heat, he rooted around and unearthed his other pair of socks. And with these on, he turned his thoughts to food. And for this he fed himself salt herring and potatoes and neeps with a cup of milk and some tea to close the meal.

Alasdair sat back, stretched his legs towards the fire, belched softly and closed his eyes. A light wind had got up and was stroking at the roof. The peats hissed, the warmth rose into the edge of the room. His head sagged and the frown of exhaustion crept across his forehead.

THE DEAD OF WINTER

Aye, An Sionnach was a bad one—aye, hellish altogether . . . but where's the point in making matters worse by chasing after the man just so as to have the chance to beat the hell out of him. There'd be no great satisfaction in that and then, by Christ, ye never knew, the wee bugger might well take it into his head to start back at me again . . . and then there'd be no end to it—no, never. But one'd think twice about helping the man again for all one got for one's trouble. . . . But there's one thing for sure—I'd no stand by and watch the man strike his woman again. No, by God, then I'd take him for sure, for yon's a fine lassy—and friendly too. . . .

And at that point, before the fire with his stomach full, his body tired and the picture of the woman rising in the curved theatre of his closed eyes, Alasdair's consciousness began to wander into the landscape of unreality. Beyond a dim shadow in the corner of his mind, he thought nothing more of An Sionnach and gave himself over to the woman. Confused memories of her ranged before him in which she appeared in many different ways. Sometimes images of her flesh, sometimes isolated gestures, sometimes the sound of her voice, but always there returned the stark features of her face.

When Alasdair awoke, the fire was petering out. Kicking off his boots and dropping his jerkin and cap on to the chair, he shuffled across the room and fell on to the bed.

9

FROM those days onwards, about a month before
the winter solstice, the land seemed to draw
itself in. The hills settled themselves lower,
hunching up their shoulders and pulling down
their heads in preparation for the period of
prolonged darkness. The sea took on a milky
viscousness, a sleepiness, as if it were on the
brink of freezing. Only the burns plundered
on as ever, though even their waters took on a
new degree of blackness. And the animal life, too,
slowed down in its daily excursions. The sheep and
the cow at Cragaig looked drugged with resignation,
spending long spells standing in one spot and
staring at the skyline, sensing the cold which lay
not so far away. Down on the shore, the occasional
heron or gull flew voicelessly with leaden wing-
beats. And gradually the temperature fell.

The slack airs of the past month were slowly
drawn taut, leaving the world about the village
tense, expectant. And then, with the early evening
darkness, there returned the frost. The cruel,
hard frost which clamped itself across the land,
splitting rocks, halting small movements of water,
killing off the less hardy of the wild animals.
And it came as it always came, not with great

flurries and demonstrations like the storms but in total silence, under cover of night, when the creatures were least prepared for it. It encircled the land, moving in over the sea and dropping out of the thin, empty sky and then ran in swiftly so that many of the weaker animals that fell in those nights scarcely had time to turn their heads before the steel cold crushed the life out of them.

For six days and nights the land was held in the vice. Each evening people went to bed earlier than usual, seeking the warmth of the blankets and their spouse's body with the numb despair of the animals and yet still found themselves only just below the surface of sleep throughout the night as the icy air bound itself about their heads. And in the morning, when they crept forth from the bed, they found the windows thick-curtained with frost and ice, their water supply frozen solid and the stone floors a penance for bare feet. Until well into the morning it was warmer outside the house than in and even by the early afternoon, when the air was at its warmest, the chairs were pulled up near the hearth.

And then, in the second week of December, the frost receded slightly and a light wind came in off the sea. But the people were still far from assured. They sniffed the air and watched the sky and talked of little else. And as the frost hovered and wavered, some of the older folk said that there was a wee bit too much north in the wind for their liking. And the others looked at them and then turned away to gaze to the north.

And sure enough, a day later, the clear sky thickened over with bluey-grey clouds and by the late afternoon the first flakes of snow had begun to fall. That first evening it fell silently and without drama and one had to press one's face up against the inky window panes to be able to see it coming down. It was generally hoped that there would be just this one evening's snow, enough to make the bairns happy and not enough to make life difficult for the men and their animals.

But during the night the snow was joined by a strong wind so that when daylight came, faces were to be seen at the windows, anxiously peering out on a scene of white desolation as the wind-blown snow was driven across the countryside. The wind roared and keened, tugging at bushes and heathers, whipping the snow already lying into whorls and spouts and for ever chasing in reinforcements from out over the sea to the north. Under the power of this onslaught, the country-side began to take on a new shape. As the snow was blown off the exposed ridges and driven into light drifts in hollows and corners, the ancient contours were slowly changed. Former depressions in the ground vanished; a flank of knotted black heathers became a dusty brown-grey, then a white-grey and finally evolved into a mould of pure white punctured by strong black sprigs.

THE DEAD OF WINTER

Small outcrops of rock which normally went unnoticed suddenly took on a new importance as their sheer sides failed to hold the snow and remained harsh spots amid fields of softness.

And throughout that day the snow continued to fall and the wind continued to blow. The bairns were allowed out to play near the house but in most cases soon came in again, smarting from the bitter cold. As dusk came, the families gathered round the fire, the men dour from the threat to their livestock, the bairns whining and obstreperous from not getting enough exercise and the women tired and irritable from having to deal with both lots of them. But at last the bairns were asleep in bed and the grown folk sat silently by the fire with their tea, listening to the blizzard outside.

The next morning the snow had stopped though a good wind still spun and chased about the countryside. But with only the cold wind to contend with the bairns went out for their fun. There were shouts and challenges and volleys of snowballs and the occasional mishap and inevitable tears when some brute was accused of loading his ammunition with stones, and it was with difficulty that they were persuaded to come in and eat their lunch, though when they did finally get to the table they fell on the food as if it were the first they had seen in a week. Early in the afternoon it began to snow again.

The snow was only light but the wind increased

in strength until the small flakes were flying almost horizontally across the land, bringing the blindness of shifting gauze about each and every house. Gradually the light dimmed into evening and still the wind and snow whistled in upon the island.

Alasdair Mór peered out from the window of his house at Cragaig. Here the snow seemed to be blowing in all directions at once for the wind brought it up the gullets, down from the hills, along the cliffs and even back up past the outhouse.

The last ten days had been depressing for him. He had got no work done and once the snow had come he had been indoors nearly all the time, only going out to give the animals their fodder. There had been little to do except try and keep warm without using too many peats and it was only out of boredom that he had done a few practical things like cleaning his rifle and burning some of the rubbish that had accumulated at the back of the building. Now, out of a need for company more than from any concern for his beasts, he put on his cap and went out, heading in the direction of the outhouse where they were closeted for the night.

He floundered along through a layer of powder snow which came up to his shins and each time his feet disturbed the snow the wind caught at the loosened powder and whirled it away in long plumes so that he left a trail of smoking footprints. He walked with his head tucked well down into his shoulders against the storm. Down below him he saw the phantom shape of the outhouse. Already an immense drift lay piled against its northern end and from this there appeared to be coming a fluttering pennant of steam as the snow was picked up by the wind.

He opened the door and slipped in. The darkness was full of the warm, acrid smell of the sheep. He struck a match and lit the lantern that hung by the door. Under its yellow glow he smiled at his beasts.

The building was divided in four. On the far left was a stall where his cow lay, champing slowly at her stock of hay with her great bistre eyes shining dolefully in the light. Separated from the cow by a rough wooden partition were the handful of sheep which had come to life with Alasdair's appearance. They milled around in anticipation, a seething mass of greasy wool and thoughtless eyes. Some bleated, some came forward hopefully towards the man and then turned and were caught up again in the throng. Undemanding friends.

Beyond another partition were stacked a number of tools—a rake, some spades, an axe, a fork and a wheelbarrow—and a good-sized pile of peats. And, at the far end of the building behind a length of wire netting were his hens in their nightly retreat which they had entered by a low door in the outer wall.

THE DEAD OF WINTER

Alasdair picked up the lantern and took it with him as he visited the animals. A moving pool of yellow light, sliced and divided by monstrous shadows from the supporting beams of the roof. In turn the various groups of animals came under the light and their eyes rolled and turned as they looked up from their rest at the man with the prickly face and converging eyes who smiled down at them, muttering and mumbling in the language of affection and concern. Outside the blizzard raged.

At last he had greeted and blessed them all, had seen them warm and at ease in their lairs of hay. He replaced the lantern, extinguished it and went out. The creatures blinked and moved restlessly for a while and then settled down to a peaceful night.

Alasdair walked uphill beneath the soft grape-shot of the blizzard, his head turned sideways, his face locked in a grimace. To arrive back inside the house and close the door was to plunge into a deep pool outside which the storm was only a muffled menace. He sat down by the fire and poured himself another cup of tea. The tea was soured but he drank it out of boredom. The peats glowed and Alasdair stared into them, mesmerised by his own lethargy after the days of inaction.

From a couple of meetings with Aulay, Alasdair had learned that as yet An Sionnach had not been seen. Aulay himself was convinced that the man

was up in the hills, hiding in one of the shepherds'
bothies and waiting for time to pass before returning to his house. Indeed it was probable that
the arrival of the snow had driven him home.
However, nobody had been near his house since
the snow started and so his whereabouts remained
unknown.

Right from the day when the frost had arrived
and the countryside had fallen under a preter-
natural stillness, Alasdair Mór had felt oddly
uneasy. It was not in the nature of this slow-
minded giant to feel uneasy and for a day or two
he had brushed it aside, passing it off as something
imagined. But the cold wore on and the stillness
lay on the land and Alasdair found himself
suddenly glancing up at the skyline or turning
round apprehensively when he was working in
the garden. As if he were expecting something—or
somebody. Repeatedly he told himself that people
rarely came out his way. And yet he still continued
to feel on edge. But he never actually saw anything and often enough laughed at himself for the
way his imagination seemed to be playing tricks
on him.

It was as if the land were on the alert, waiting
for something. The action of the storms and high
winds had all given way to a calm where every
slightest sound was taken up by the echoes,
where any movement was noticed. And under the
frost the land seemed drained, empty. So that
when Alasdair had met Aulay one afternoon in

the middle of the cold spell it seemed as if they were the last two people in that corner of the earth. Numbed by the vicious cold, there was nothing to feel, nothing to hear, nothing to see. Alasdair mentioned to Aulay that there was something uncanny in the air but Aulay obviously did not know what he was talking about and so he returned to Cragaig more than ever convinced that it was all in his imagination. And yet, in spite of this, he still glanced about him with covered eyes and pressed his pace onwards towards the setting sun.

Each day he was up early, snapped from a shallow sleep by the nipping air. He sat on the edge of the bed, sipping a cup of tea and listening. From time to time there was a sound of movement from the fire but otherwise there was little but the sounds of his own body—the sucking in of the hot liquid and the gulp as it went down his throat; the rubbing of material as he shifted his shoulders against the cold; the puffing sound and the twisting plume before him as he breathed out; the sudden grinding of his tackety boots on the stone floor. And then, in the heart of the nervous silence, the sound of irregular steps on the stone flags by the door, only slowly identifying themselves as those of a grazing sheep. Winter solitude.

And so it was that when the snows came, they brought Alasdair Mór a sense of relief, for in the last days of the frost he had begun to long for the sound of the wind in the village and the sight of

his beloved coast brought back to life. With the
first stirrings of the wind which preceded the
snow, it seemed to Alasdair that the tension was
passing, that the inexplicable shadow was lifting.
And then the snow itself followed, sweeping in on
the wind across the village of Cragaig with un-
abated vigour and to all appearance, blotting out
the frozen ground and the disquiet of the past
days. But the snow in its flat, perspectiveless
dimensions is a deceiver.

After that one brief morning when the bairns
had got out to play, the wind had carried back
the snow in the early afternoon and for hour
after hour it continued. It was in the evening of
that day that Alasdair had paid his late visit to
the animals and then retired with his tea to the
hearth. It was close on an hour that he sat there
kicking his heels but then he got up, pushed a few
things aside and prepared for bed. He took a last
look out on the driving snow, blew out the lamp
and climbed on to the bed.

But it was more apathy than genuine tiredness
that had made him go to bed and so he just lay
there wide awake, the last flames of the fire
casting leaping shadows about the near end of the
room, the wind crying and groaning round the
building and throwing the crystals of snow up
against the windows with a soft pattering. His
mind wandered flightily from thought to thought.
With the warmth of bed and the light of the fire
about him it was a pleasure to hear the blustering

of the blizzard outside. And quite suddenly he was asleep.

He awoke, half sitting up. The fire was out and the room black. The wind had raised its cry and was now hammering into the walls and whistling about the chimney and roof. Why had he woken like that, so abruptly, as if somebody had tapped him on the shoulder? Then he remembered. He had been dreaming that he was over at the autumn sales on the mainland. They had been at the cattle market when all of a sudden every single one of the beasts in the pens had opened its throat and released a wild, desperate bellow. Alasdair lay back on the bed and drew the blankets tight about himself. What a strange dream! And the twining howls of the wind began to run over him again and he slipped backwards into a state of half consciousness. As he started to drop off to sleep, he heard on the fluctuations of the wind a noise like a hammer striking wood.

Deep into the night the wind and snow poured through Cragaig, laying a good foot of snow on the level ground and building drifts and mounds so that it looked as if a small herd of large beasts had fallen asleep and been covered. But at some stage in the small hours the snowfall thinned and then stopped; and soon after, the wind too began to slacken. By daybreak, only a capricious breeze flickered about the hollow.

When Alasdair first stirred in the grey shadows of his house, he became slowly aware that the noise which he heard was not part of a dream but was actually coming from nearby. He blinked a couple of times and turned on to his back. The timbers of the roof hung above him.

It was an irregular sound like a hammer striking wood and for a while he was unable to place it. Then he realised that it was no more than the door of the outhouse banging in the wind. It must have blown open during the night. He had best go down and make sure that the animals were all right.

As he ate his breakfast, Alasdair wandered about peering out of the windows time and again at the early morning scene. Across what he could see of the village from his windows, the thin citric streaks of the rising sun shone on the deep snow. He finished his tea and went out.

Around the sunrise the sky was already taking on a blue tinge but nearer the sun itself, whose edge had just crept over the rim of the hills, it glared, a flaxen metal, so that Alasdair had to shield his eyes against it. The hills themselves were a complex of light and darkness as the sunlight caught the upper shoulders, putting their deep cushioned fields of snow into explosions of brightness while the lower slopes lay black and blue-white in the last clutches of the night. Everywhere the snow stretched; everywhere its lithe form spread over the sleeping land. This was not the year's death but a fulfilment of peace for in the skin of whiteness lay no threats of

dark and cold but the drugged warmth and light
of the coming spring. Below the impassive mask-
ing, the new year's harvest lay breathing softly.

Closer to the village Alasdair saw the thin
stalks of old brackens, of reeds, of grasses which
now looked out of place, as if they had been
planted like pins in a cushion. And he saw too
how the snow had forced an entry everywhere.
The crevices of the walls were mortared with it;
the great ash tree's northern sides and joints were
plastered with it; even the gable end of a ruin,
pointing north, had a deep drift of it piled on the
inner side. Out on the hillock its weight was
supported on the springs of the heathers. And now
the whole scene was beginning to flare up under
the sun's rays, which hurried and shot and
ricocheted off the burnished surface. Through a
dip, the far off sea showed itself blue-grey milk
beneath the receding night.

Alasdair marvelled and smiled at the sight.
Then, humming huskily, he floundered thoughtfully down towards the outhouse. The crystals of
snow jumped and sparkled like stars of dizziness
before him. At each step, a spray of powder
billowed out like surf.

The wind had dropped and the outhouse door
hung ajar. And as he put his hand on the door he
knew that something had happened. In that
moment, just before he pushed the door open, his
breathing paused. It was like a thin sliver of ice
grazing against his heart. But he pushed the door

open and went in. In the few seconds of his sight
adjusting to the half-light, he did not understand
what he saw. Then the odd shapes and colours and
the comprehension of the complete silence slid
into reality.

The building contained a scene of repulsive
chaos. Before him, as he stood nailed in the doorway, his flock of sheep lay heaped and scattered,
now hardly more than an indecipherable mass of
wool and blood and entrails. The carcasses lay in
confusion, seemingly frozen in the act of falling.
Legs stuck rigidly into the air from beneath the
bellies of other beasts; a pair of eyes stared
glaucously from a blood-soaked head that seemed
to grow from another sheep's haunch; one sheep
lay on its back, its head hanging out of sight, its
four legs standing up like antennae, its belly
split open by a terrible gash from which there
oozed and bulged the complexities of its guts. It
was almost as if the animal were in the process of
exploding. Each and every one of the sheep was
marked by deep, gaping cuts that exposed bone
and flesh. In one case the head was only just
attached to the body by a few sinews, some
fearsome blow having been placed deep in the
fleece of the neck.

In the enclosure where the hens lived the scene
was no less horrible. Each one of his brood had
been caught, held fast and had a leg severed
high up across the thigh. Cast back on the ground
again it would have flapped and squawked

pathetically and scratched at the earth with its other leg while the blood spurted forth from the opened artery. The floor was nothing but a mass of round, mutilated bodies with obscene stumps. And everywhere blood, feathers and feet.

But the worst remained to be seen. Up in the stall at the other end of the building lay the cow. It had allowed itself to be turned round so that its head was towards the wall and there it was tethered by the halter which normally hung on the back of the door. The animal lay slumped on its right side with its head twisted upwards by the short halter, its eyes bulging in terror and shock. And from the bottom of its neck there protruded a long wooden handle. Alasdair recognised his axe. The head of the instrument was almost buried in the cow's flesh and what little of it that still showed was virtually submerged in a welter of gore that had spread and coagulated in a vast delta across the shoulder. And as if this had not been enough, the animal's udder had been slashed and torn by vicious strokes with a knife. The building reeked sweetly of destruction.

Alasdair wandered back and forth, his mouth hanging open vacantly, his eyes shifting from side to side, rubbing at his lower lip with the back of his great hand. He walked faster and faster as if his self-control were winding itself up like a spring. Alternately his hands scratched at his legs and rubbed at his mouth. For some minutes he kept on walking like this and then he stopped suddenly by the carcass of his cow. He stared at it with bulging eyes and shaking lips. Slowly he sank to his knees and emitting a long, baleful groan he dropped his head on to his well-loved beast's side. His hands held fast to the shaggy brown hair.

He stayed like this for a long time, mumbling incoherently into the dead cow's hide, snatches of his old milking songs breaking out and then dying as he thought of some of those evenings in the midst of the last summer's heat. With his eyes closed and his mind barricaded against the horrible slaughter about him, he drifted off into a void of unreality. He thought only of his cow and recalled the animal's docile expression and the sound of her hoofs in the mud when he fetched her for the evening milking; and the time of her first calving and the difficulties of milking her while the calf was at her too and the need for a button of rowan to hobble her; and the time she had wandered and got herself caught in the bog up in the Coire nam Fiadh and how he had heard her bellowing in fear and run up to get her out, with the ropes about her and himself laughing and cursing. . . . What a friendship had grown between them in those four years! And he raised his head from her side and looked once up at her big eyes, now charged with terror. His features were cold with misery, his eyes pinched and starting like those of a frightened child, his jaw hanging inanely.

THE DEAD OF WINTER

Getting up, he glanced again at his cow, shuffled around uselessly by the heapings of fleece and limbs and sprouting entrails that had been his flock of sheep and then, as if the true horror of what lay before him were only just beginning to dawn on him, he fumbled for the catch on the door and half fell out into the bright sunlight.

He stood there by the doorway, up to his calves in snow, with little splatters and streaks of red and brown blood discolouring his footprints behind him. He stood there bending forward with his hands on his knees and his head hanging low as if he were about to vomit. Indeed he coughed and spat and dribbled as his stomach rebelled against him and when eventually he straightened up his face was grey under the week's stubble.

He stared blankfaced before him at the ash tree in the garden, Its lower branches, on which it rested, plunged deep in the snow. The wind scurried hither and thither, plucking at the surface of the snow and whirling it away in miniature storms. Otherwise nothing moved. Nothing suffered with Alasdair. The world was bright and full of joy. He alone in that winter garden knew of the scene in the outhouse; he alone must carry the agony of the world gone wrong. He took a few paces to the left, then a few to the right, his arms dangling by his sides like useless limbs. He stopped again and stared at the snow by his feet. Alasdair Mór felt himself broken.

Yet the mechanisms of his mind clicked slowly onwards and now he wondered what other injuries had been laid on him. The savage attack on his animals had been directed at him, at his possessions. . . . His boat? He moved off again making his way to the cliff, wading laboriously through the banks of snow.

He ploughed along, kneading his fists together, his eyes straying sleepily over the ground in front of him. His steps were slow, as if he had lost interest, as if the matter of his boat were no longer of any concern. He even stopped occasionally and stood stock still in the midst of the cold wastes for several minutes. Then he started off again, but ponderously, purposelessly.

It took him almost twice as long as usual to get to Port nam Freumh. On the way down the cliff he passed through drifts that came up to his waist so that by the time he reached the shore the lower half of his body was encrusted with bobbles of snow and ice. When he at last reached the harbour and saw his boat lying calmly at its moorings, its benches covered by fat strips of snow, there was no sign of rejoicing or relief on his face. He kept hanging his head and shaking it from side to side as he refused to accept what he still knew to be true, all the while moving his fingers and hands nervously.

Although the boat itself was untouched, the oars had gone but it only took a few minutes of desultory searching for him to find the remains of a fire in a corner among the rocks. The small container of paraffin had been taken from the outhouse and brought down to make a good fire out of the oars and a dozen lobster boxes. In among the ashes Alasdair found the blackened remains of a hen's leg and the half of an oar's blade, charred and discoloured. Under the rocks by the fire, lay an empty whisky bottle.

But all this appeared to have no effect on him. He rooted around with his boot in the ashes and then, picking up the remains of the blade, walked out to the end of the jetty and sat down.

As he sat there looking out on to the fields of the ocean, Alasdair gradually began to clear his mind of the mists of shock. He saw, first, the scene in the byre the night before. The man letting himself in under the cover of the storm, lighting the small lantern and methodically going about his task. The cow which had been turned and tethered first. Meanwhile the sheep would have been moving around nervously, unsure of this midnight stranger. But it would not have been long before the man appeared in front of them, axe in hand and swaying slightly from the drink. After the first few blows, the blood lust would have been up and the deed completed with the swiftness of frenzy. When they had been finished, the hens would have been dealt with. And finally his cow. She would have been straining at the halter by now, driven almost out of her mind by the fearful noises and the ever growing stench of death from over the partition. Then a grim silence, broken only by the last twitchings of the other animals and the sound of the footsteps stealthily approaching her from behind. She would have heaved and bellowed but the man knew what he was about and first the knife slashed and ripped and then, as her hind legs buckled under her, the swish of the axe.

Alasdair closed his eyes again and pressed the blackened piece of wood against his forehead. There was a certain relief in the pressure of something solid against the cold skin of his skull. As the anguish of the scene in the village dissolved, his mind began to roam over the events of the past two months. Only two months! And before that the decades of his life when nobody had bothered about him and he had bothered about nobody. And then the man had arrived, as if from nowhere, and set up round the corner with his woman. And while Alasdair had continued to fish as he had done for near on thirty years, the man was starting to build up this hatred, this fury against him. First there had been the creels, then the theft of his boat and now this savagery . . . for Christ's sake, what did the man want? Why did he not come and attack Alasdair himself rather than inflict his twisted anger on the helpless animals? And why did he not show himself, why did he lurk in the hills, why did he not come and face Alasdair. . . .? Oh, his poor beasts! his own and best! his family! The few creatures in his life which were his true friends, who did not treat him as a half-wit, an oddity—and now they were nothing but a mess of pulped flesh and shattered bone! Oh, the whoor of a man! the black bugger!

And, little by little, Alasdair's soul returned to life. To begin with there were few signs externally to indicate what was happening to him, to show that the great man, the sole survivor of time's hate against the village of Cragaig, was being forced back into the battle by the first spasms of mad anger stirring in his heart. He still sat there, twisting the piece of wood round and round in his hands, pressing it against his forehead, taking it away, pressing it back again, oblivious of everything about him, aware only of what was happening to him. Minute after minute went by, with the water lapping at his feet and the snow-plaided hills hanging high above him. The small world was watching, waiting to see the man make his next move.

Again Alasdair thought of his beasts and groaned. Again he thought of the evil of the man who had killed them. Again he felt the bubbling aggression of a man taunted and provoked beyond endurance. His hands trembled, his neck stiffened, his shoulders began to rise. His head rolled against the charcoal edge of the wood and he started to groan. The sound slipped out of the barrel of his chest, stopped and then started again louder. As he groaned, his fists clenched till his knuckles were bloodless white spines and then, suddenly, as if some restraint, some shackle had split loose inside him, he released a wild roar and sank his teeth deep into the charcoaly wood.

He held his grip on the wood for a second or two with noises of crunching and splintering and then, in one movement, cast the wood aside and threw back his head. The skin was drained of blood and covered in charcoal and the face was that of an old man, but his eyes—the eyes of the man!—were hard, shining stones. Only one consideration ruled him now. That of revenge.

10

IT WAS mid-morning by the time Alasdair arrived
back at Cragaig. By then, this small rim of the
Western Highlands was showing a new side to
its character for, under the sunlight, the vast
expanses of snow and ice were giving off volleys
and crackings of fire and energy. Each movement that Alasdair made touched off new detona-
tions, the whole extent of his view from the
cliffs to the high hills sparking and flaring so
violently that it was impossible for him to keep
his eyes open to it. As he twisted and turned and
lowered his head in an attempt to protect himself
from the ebullient onslaught, it looked as though
he were being driven to the brink of capitulation.
The unresting aggression of the light gave no
quarter and even as he turned this way and that
he only opened himself to new bombardments.
Yet he never slowed but marched on with determination into the depths of this phosphorescing
sea.

Though his eyes screwed up and his mouth
twisted in a weird grin from the power of the
sunlight on the snow, Alasdair Mór scarcely paid
attention to the wild splendour of the winter
morning. For his mind was planning other things—

what he would need to take with him, which way he would go, how he would set about tracking down the man.

The effect of the morning's events had been to thrust him violently downwards to a level of despair, humiliation and misery that he had never before experienced. From this pit he had been reborn, in the moment of that hideous cry, as another man, a man whose thoughts had little in common with those of the Alasdair Mór of the past. No longer did he think back nostalgically to the calm of his fisherman's life, no longer did he feel himself threatened or preyed upon, for he now was the hunter, the hunter who did not care to rest until his quarry was down. The pressures put upon him by An Sionnach's treacheries had accumulated unseen until, with this last and cruellest incursion, he had found himself cornered and finally driven out into the voids of unreason. For the past months he had regarded An Sionnach's enmity with the quiescence and passivity of a man whom years of privation had taught acceptance and resignation. But then, in the space of a few hours, the shock of the slaughter had brought to life in him the dormant but deep-seated brute instincts that support a man's need for survival. And these had taken over his being.

The winter was moving into its harshest months and commonsense would have told him that he must look to his future, that somehow he must find ways of replacing his livestock. But such commonsense never entered Alasdair's head, for each breath that he took was dominated by his urgent desire to kill An Sionnach.

He moved quickly, loping along where the thinner snow permitted and wading with an unbending rhythm through the drifts and open places. Occasionally, he cast a squinted eye up at the sun, checking the course of the day against his plans. When he came down into Cragaig he made straight for his house and, once inside, he set about his preparations with an efficiency unusual for him. He crammed his old canvas piece-bag with all the food he could lay hands on—dried fish, cheese, bread, dulse, and sugar—and then slipped into his pocket a few shillings and the six rifle bullets that remained to him. Then he rolled up the larger of his two blankets, cast the bundle over his shoulder and, picking up the rifle, went out.

He threw one wild look towards the outhouse and then stepped over the village wall and was on his way.

Although the night's drifting snow would certainly have covered An Sionnach's footprints, Alasdair felt sure that he would have made for the hills behind Achateny. For certain, he would not have gone home to his woman nor stayed in the hills between his house and Cragaig. Both of these were too near for any safety. Neither would he have gone along the road where there were a number of houses and where he would have risked being seen. And so it seemed that he must have crossed the road and headed out across the hills towards the other side of the island. For there in the hills was a tract of country, caught between two distant roads, that stretched for miles in every direction and was as desolate as any part of the island. The country there was a mass of hills and small mountains, pitted with numerous glens and corries and visited only a few times a year by the shepherds. There An Sionnach could conceal himself only too easily; but Alasdair was counting on the fact that so long as the snow lasted the man would have to leave a clear trail of footprints.

Alasdair was covering the ground with uncommon speed. He moved with an effortless urgency, one hand steadying the bundle on his shoulder, the other holding the rifle and all the while his eyes swung back and forth over the land, seeking some sign of An Sionnach's passing. But he saw no trace of the man.

Soon he was down to the road at the place where he normally met Aulay. The even carpeting of snow that lay on the road was unbroken except for the tracks of a cart and the hoof marks of its horse. Nowhere was there any sign of human footprints.

He prowled up and down the road like a ranging wolf, hurrying along and then stopping to cast around for clues before moving off once more. He came on the split-fork tracks of birds, the pad marks of rabbits and hares but never anything more. About half a mile down the road to Achateny, he was just about to move off and try elsewhere when he came to an abrupt halt, peered at the snow and then snapped upright, his eyes snaking out in pursuit of a spoor. He had him.

The footprints came down off the hills to the south of Cragaig, crossed the road and headed out into the open country of the hinterland. With a bound, Alasdair passed over the road and on to the plateau of snow-covered peat-moss that stretched for half a mile before rising into the lower slopes of the hills. The hunt was on.

Now his body rolled and swung as he padded along the thin line of the tracks. His breathing came heavily, his nose snuffled and screwed up and for ever his tackety boots thumped down on the neat footprints that climbed and dived across the ditches and furrows of the peat-moss. He kept only half an eye on the tracks for he was scanning the hills for a glimpse of An Sionnach. But the hills stood solid and bare, immense featureless backs of whiteness, pricked and dotted with a few rocks and the infrequent clump of small trees or deep heathers. On the right—to the south—they rose to the heights of Meall nan Each, a squat massif surrounded by a ring of crags and steep rocks where a pair of eagles nested. Peering over the southern slopes of Meall nan Each, the distant crown of Sidhean na

Raplaich pushed itself, white and shaped, into the clear sky.

It seemed that Alasdair was in luck for the sky was empty of snow clouds and the land lay encased below a tent of watered blue that attached itself to the horizon by a hem of light, glowing like an ice blink. It would freeze hard the night, Alasdair thought to himself, but no bother in that so long as the footprints stayed.

He stormed on for an hour or more and gradually the furious drive of his body cooled and he settled into a changeless trotting that took him deep into the hills. His mind, too, had sloughed off the madness and reeling passions of misery and had been tempered to a sullen hardness. The emotions of the early morning had collected into a hard knot of resolve. Though these hours of uneventful travelling through the snow had worn down the excited anticipation of getting to grips with An Sionnach, the desire to see his animals avenged lay unquenchable within him. Indeed, it was the memory of their deaths that endlessly spurred him forwards, driving him up banks and corries through thigh-deep snow and plunging him down again in pursuit of the empty footprints that curled and wound before him.

It soon became clear that An Sionnach had made for the bothy that lay at the back of Leac Shoilleir, opposite Beinn na Cille. Winding in and out of the small glens, Alasdair eventually followed the tracks around a shallow cliff and

saw the hut wedged in a hollow a short way along
the hillside. He slipped back and stood in the
shadow of the cliff from where he could still see
the hut. Its roof, hung with snow, protruded
sleepingly from the bulging sail of the slope.
Nothing moved. Nothing showed. Alasdair
glanced up at the higher ridges, their edges
crispate against the filtered blue of the sky. All
emptiness: a desolation that seemed to have never
known the intrusions of men.

For a while longer he waited but seeing no
sign of life, he retraced his steps and went up the
back of the spur in order to come down on the
building from above. When he reached the top he
searched the opposing hills but the dazzling
mottle of bright light and shadow put an impenetrable mask over the scene. So, loading
the rifle, he slunk forward over the edge and
made down on the bothy. Still nothing moved
and the only sound on the air was the
crunching and squeaking of his boots compressing
the snow.

Stealthily he came round to the front of the
building where the snow lay trampled and dirty.
He paused a moment and then, slipping the catch,
he barged in. The thick light hissed with silence
and threw up its rancid, bitter smells of old
fleeces. A wide bench stood against the far wall.
A few empty bottles and cigarette packets
littered the floor. A small pile of sheep's wool lay
in a corner. And the sunlight, reflecting off the

ground outside, seeped into the room, slipping past Alasdair's bulky frame in the doorway.

Alasdair breathed out deeply and walked in. He looked quickly around and then his sight fell on an old lid of a tin on the bench. It had been used as an ashtray and in it there was a half-smoked cigarette. Alasdair picked it up and felt it. It was firm and dry. An Sionnach could not be long gone. When he looked up, Alasdair's face was alive with new hope.

He threw down the cigarette, picked up his rifle and made for the door. The brightness outside hit him across the face, stunned him to blindness for a few seconds. High above the top of Leac Shoilleir a buzzard cried and the sound of life in the frozen glen was startlingly clear so that Alasdair turned towards the bird. Its cross-head form swung on a spiral pivot as it rose motionless into the faceless sky. Again it cried and the sounding despair of this solitary creature far out in the unstirring ocean of the air held Alasdair in a momentary memory of his life at Cragaig, with the cliffs where he alone walked. But it was only a brief relapse in his imperturbable resolve, the twitchings of a deep-rooted joy, for as he watched the sailing bird, he saw the thin shape of a man appear on the skyline below it. The man halted and stood with his hands on his hips, looking down towards Alasdair and the bothy.

Alasdair's breath caught in his throat. Without moving, he slipped off the safety catch on the rifle. The two men stood facing each other while the bird flew round and round above. Then, in one swift movement, Alasdair swung the rifle to his shoulder, aimed and fired. The whipsound tore through the veils of icy silence and was answered and swallowed by a pack of short echoes. The man on the ridge snatched at his arm and went over backwards. The buzzard flapped its wings briefly and turned away south. The silence poured back into the glen.

Alasdair emptied the breech, adjusted the blanket on his shoulder, hawked and spat and then set off vigorously up the side of Leac Shoilleir. A look of malicious satisfaction covered his face. He bounded up through the snow, putting all his strength into the climb for he knew that if he were quick he might take the man before he could recover from the wound. But the distance was deceptive and the snow held him back so that it was a good while before he came out on the level of the ridge, just below the top of the hill. He was puffing and blowing from the effort and his face was crossed by lines of sweat but he never paused and went straight out along the slender spine. He came to the small area of disturbed snow where An Sionnach had stood and saw, just behind it, the pit which his body had made as it fell beneath the rifle shot. A sharp flash of blood lay like a brightly coloured rag on the white surface. But of the man himself there was no sign.

Behind the ridge the ground fell into a deep corrie where a small burn ran. From the patch of blood there were signs that An Sionnach had rolled and slithered down into the corrie, crossed the burn and made off up the other side. Alasdair grasped his rifle and sprang down the slope.

With his considerable weight Alasdair descended at great speed, bounding and skiing as his feet slid forwards so that he appeared to travel with gigantic strides. Somehow he managed to keep his balance and came to a halt with a neat skid by the edge of the water. Before him, An Sionnach's tracks climbed skywards and vanished over the next crest. He crossed the burn and began to work his way laboriously up the other side, cursing and storming as he struggled to lift his feet clear of the deep snow. Every now and again he noticed spots of blood, absorbed and turned to a rusty opaqueness by the cold crystals.

Reaching the top, he looked down on a wide hillside, intersected by another burn, and out into a large glen. The head of this glen was made by the ridge and eastern slopes of Leac Shoilleir—where Alasdair now stood—but gradually it opened out between the hills of Sidhean na Raplaich and Meall nan Each. On meeting the valley bed, the burn that he had just crossed and the one that stood before him both turned south, joined and developed into a young river that flowed in ever growing force down the glen away through the distant hills.

THE DEAD OF WINTER

From his vantage point Alasdair commanded a view of the whole glen and his eyes tensed and shone as he surveyed the open space for An Sionnach. But there was no sign of him either on the slopes or in the glen below. Where the hell had the bugger got to? From where Alasdair stood, the tracks led diagonally down the hill to meet the burn some two hundred yards below him. Beyond the burn there were no visible traces. Something was wrong. And beyond the burn the countryside lay open with little or no cover. With the sun at its early afternoon angle the glen was filled with brightness. Way down the near slope a hare stood poised on a rise.

Alasdair frowned and then followed on in the tracks. No signs of blood any more. The footprints ran to the edge of the burn and then stopped. On the far bank the snow lay moulded and pure. Alasdair paused and used the blanket to wipe the sweat from his face. Again he looked before him into the glen. Then he looked back to where he had come from and saw the thick furrow in the snow that the two of them had made, now blued and inked in by the shadows that lay in each depression. Well, by Christ, yon's a hell of a canny! Alasdair's thoughts were sliding into darkness.

But something made him turn and look up the burn. And there at the top, near the summit of Leac Shoilleir, stood An Sionnach. He was standing as he had stood on the ridge, cut out against the weak colour of the sky, immobile, a perfect target for a rifle shot. There was something insolent in the way that he stood waiting: something brazen-faced and taunting, so that Alasdair's head span with another flood of anger, of pride humiliated.

'The cheeky wee bugger!' Alasdair's face hardened into the stone features of ill-concealed fury but even as he raised his weapon An Sionnach was away over the skyline and Alasdair was left with a pounding heart and an empty hillside.

As he stumbled upwards he realised that An Sionnach had played on him one of the oldest tricks of the chase. He had headed down to the burn to give the impression that he was making for the glen but had then doubled back uphill splashing and wading up the burn until he had got high enough for his tracks not to be visible from below. All this Alasdair could see and understand. But why the man should choose to play this game of tantalising him, he could not begin to understand. Any normal man would have kept moving as fast as possible and tried to put as much ground between himself and his pursuer in the hope of shaking him off. . . . And so Alasdair puzzled at it to himself as he stamped higher and higher into the snows, his uncomplicated mind trying to fathom out the problem in his own terms.

That afternoon the chase continued hour after hour in the same manner. Some times An Sionnach would seem to be almost in his grasp before managing to wriggle free; at other times, it was as if An Sionnach had simply gone to earth and Alasdair wandered about, for ever mouthing mumbled curses in his unimaginative invective, waiting for the man to appear again. And appear again he always did, in his insolent manner, allowing Alasdair time enough to see him but making sure that he dropped out of sight before Alasdair could take a shot at him. In this way he contrived to egg Alasdair on, dragging him in his wake as if he did not want him to give up, implying some plan, some method in his odd behaviour. And he was as canny as his name suggested, using every trick and deceit to keep out of the older man's grasp. In addition, his lighter build and the fact that he was not encumbered by a gun or a blanket meant that he could travel faster than Alasdair.

He led Alasdair back up on to Leac Shoilleir, around the shoulder that joined it to Meall nan Each, south along the summit ridge of that hill and then round and back along its eastern flank. As the sun set and the open glen where Alasdair had first lost him fell under the dead colourings of the evening light, Alasdair caught the day's last glimpse of An Sionnach. The man was far to the north of him, a silhouette against the yellowing sky, fighting his way through the snows of the very ridge of Leac Shoilleir where he had fallen to Alasdair's shot some four hours earlier. At the top of the climb, he turned for a moment and then vanished into the glen where the bothy lay.

By now Alasdair was tired and he realised that even with the moonlight he would gain little by trying to pursue An Sionnach by night. So he tramped wearily back up over the hill and headed down for the smudge of dark that was the bothy. An Sionnach would not risk going there for the night and so Alasdair decided that he had best make use of the only building in the area for the night hours. As he walked down to the cold, bleak hut his spirits were low.

When Alasdair had started out from Cragaig that morning he had gone with the blind determination of the hunter; the hunter not of glory but of a species of malignant vermin. He had gone in anger, in righteousness to settle the matter once and for all. The Highland spirit, the pride of the independent man, was resurrected in him. Gone were the unquestioning resignation, the little considered acceptance of his hardships and poverty, for he had risen from this torpor to seek vengeance. It never crossed his mind to take the matter to the authorities of the law—the attack had been against him, against his standing and he alone could gain the reparation he desired. He went forth with that spirit of sullen anger that he had seen in his own grandfather when the old man had spoken of the Clearances.

But as the day had worn on and An Sionnach had tricked and escaped him time and again his feelings had started to change. He, the hunter, the one to be feared, was mocked. So often did An Sionnach vanish only to appear again a few minutes later in some unlikely spot that Alasdair began to feel that he himself was the hunted one, that An Sionnach was the man in command. And yet, in ways, this very reversal, this constant humiliation, served to drive him deeper into his resolve. Constantly he recalled the scene in the byre and how the man had wilfully turned his spite on him. And each time these thoughts came to him, he put aside a bit more of his pride, his self-esteem. So that by the time he came back to the bothy under the light of the ailing day, his frame of mind had dropped to that of a wild animal. Now nothing was too low for him, no course of action too mean. He who had always treated others so fairly, who had lived and let live in unthinking honesty and generosity. All considerations for himself and for others were put aside. He thought only of the kill.

That night Alasdair Mór was to find little peace. By the light of a candle which he found in the bothy he fed himself on the scraps of food from his piece-bag. Then he blew out the candle and settled himself down on the bench under his blanket, using his piece-bag as a pillow. The rifle stood by his side.

The night was still and cold. Alasdair wondered where An Sionnach had taken himself to. Probably to one of the caves among the rocks of

Meall nan Each which the animals used for shelter on wild nights. Alasdair's mind never stopped turning over the events the day and the possibilities that lay ahead. . . . If An Sionnach's intention was to leave the island, he would have done so by now. If his original intention had been just to lie low for a while but had changed to a plan of escape when he had seen Alasdair's anger, why had he continued to move round in circles all afternoon and not made off across the country? And if he had no plan of escape, what was he thinking on doing? And yet, inexplicably, Alasdair knew that when the morrow came he would find An Sionnach close at hand. . . .

He lay there in the darkness, staring wide-eyed into the bottomless pit of the night, his face twitching and twisting with the pressures in his mind. His fingers fidgeted beneath the blanket. He moved about trying to find some comfort in the hard boards of the bench. . . . Perhaps Alasdair Mór was afraid. Afraid not of the man, the man who toyed with him as a cat with a mouse, but afraid of the riddles of the situation, afraid when he had those long hours to think about something which he could not understand. Whatever it may have been, Alasdair spent much of that hard, silent night stretched sleeplessly on the bench and it was with relief that he finally got up in the first glimmerings of the new day.

Huddled miserably in the corner of the building he ate the remains of his food by candlelight and

was ready to leave when the rays of the early
sun were throwing into silhouette the smooth
outline of Beinn na Cille.

The day broke still and clear, with the snow
crusted and sharp from the night's frost. Its icy
surface crackled and crunched beneath the weight
of Alasdair's boots as he walked away from the
bothy and headed for the summit of Leac Shoilleir. With no definite idea of where An Sionnach
might be, Alasdair thought it best to get himself
early to a good view point so that he could
watch the countryside as the daylight grew.
From Leac Shoilleir he would be able to see the
glens to the north and south and the slopes of both
Meall nan Each and Sidhean na Raplaich.

When he came out on top he felt warmer from
the climb and his spirits were better. At that
moment the landscape lay on the very edge of the
day. Arms and scallop-shells of oily sunlight
struck and soared off the other side of the hills,
leaving the glens beneath Alasdair's feet wadded
with icy shadows and patches of darkness. Here
and there on the hills about him little points and
crags, laced with shreds of snow, were caught by
the light as it slipped through some high pass.
Alasdair leant on his rifle and prepared to wait.

It was about three-quarters of an hour later,
when his side of the glens was coming under the
sunlight, that Alasdair saw a small figure detach
itself from the lower slopes at the other end of
Meall nan Each and head rapidly out across the

glen to the small river. There was little chance of a shot at that distance so Alasdair dropped to one knee and watched to see where the man would go. Within yards, An Sionnach was into the shadows of Sidhean na Raplaich. Crossing the river he turned slightly leftwards and made for the opening of the steep gullet that separated Sidhean na Raplaich and Beinn na Cille. From the general direction of his route, Alasdair surmised that An Sionnach was, after all, going to make off eastwards across the island.

Like a startled animal, Alasdair was off and slinking along the ridge and into the freezing shadows. He traversed the hill and came out near the foot of the gullet just as An Sionnach crawled out at the top. Before he vanished from sight, An Sionnach turned and saw Alasdair below him and straightaway he was gone. Today he was in flight.

Up the gullet Alasdair came, his head surrounded by small clouds of steam as his breath poured out on to the chill air. He slipped and fell on to his elbows in the deep snow and as he got to his feet he looked up and saw the sagging bag of the gullet's head filled to the brim with the white sky. Again he started to climb, pushing up through that enclosure, that tunnel of shadows where sounds reverberated and where the air was crossed with reflections of the snow's night-time coldness.

At the moment that his head broke out at the top, Alasdair felt his energies and hopes refired

by the bursting sunlight that came flooding and
charging across the hills to the east. But it was to
the east that An Sionnach's escape route must
lie if he were to catch one of the mainland boats;
and in that direction everything lay blotted out
by sheens of dazzling light as the low-slung sun
came clear of the hills.

Alasdair attempted to combat the dazzle and
then, dropping his eyes, decided that he would do
best to follow the tracks for the moment. And
straightaway, he was on to the day's first dis-
illusionment. An Sionnach's tracks, instead of
continuing east, turned abruptly northwards along
the back of Beinn na Cille. And in that direction,
at the edge of the hills, lay the road between
Achateny and the town, and the sea. What, in
God's name, was the man away to now? But
there was no time to waste in standing about and
thinking, for each moment An Sionnach would be
pulling away. So Alasdair set off in hot pursuit,
following the footprints that cut across the
hollows of the hill.

Some minutes later, he caught sight of An
Sionnach rising from a section of dead ground
and making up over a rise. Alasdair quickly
drew the rifle up to his shoulder and just had time
to put in a shot. But An Sionnach, by some
uncanny intuition, swung left as the bullet sped
on its way and, with no more than a puff of snow
as the surface was disturbed, the man thrust hard
and was away over the top.

THE DEAD OF WINTER

As Alasdair continued his fruitless chase across the hills, the sun grew steadily warmer. Then, unannounced, the first touches of a wind caught him on the cheek and he glanced up immediately for it had come from the southwest. The next time he rose to a high point he looked down in the direction of the wind and saw, as he expected, that the southwestern horizon was heavy with stacks of cloud. It would not be long before the rain came. By some means, he must take An Sionnach soon.

Around midday, the two men came to the northern edge of the hills. Through the morning the agile, younger man had opened up a good lead on his hunter and so it was with confidence that he set off across the short snowy plain that lay bordered, on the far side, by the road. On this part of the flats, the land was dotted with numerous rocks and little mounds that rose beneath the snow like bubbles of trapped air. Across the plain and just beyond the road stood the uneven shape of Beinn Chreagach, the mountain that lay only a mile to the north of Cragaig.

When Alasdair reached the end of the hills, he looked down on the plain and saw An Sionnach zig-zagging away among the rocks and hillocks. Never in the hours of the chase had he had An Sionnach before him in such open ground. In a frenzy of excitement and re-awakened anger, Alasdair dropped the blanket and took up a stance behind a rock.

THE DEAD OF WINTER

The next time that An Sionnach moved out from cover Alasdair carefully took aim and fired. The shot rang out with a barking harshness and An Sionnach stumbled and went sprawling forwards into the snow. Alasdair snorted with triumph and the sunlight caught the sparkle of satisfaction in his eyes. But then his face darkened in a frown. An Sionnach was scrambling to his feet and running, bent double, one arm hanging limply at his side. By coincidence, the shot had taken him as before, high in the left arm.

Cursing again, Alasdair reloaded and set off down the gentle slope, springing powerfully with his old strength now that he had An Sionnach at his mercy. But An Sionnach had not just collapsed behind some rock for he reappeared again, with some white cloth as a tourniquet around his arm, running as hard as ever for the next cover. And now he scarcely halted, scuttling from rock to hillock and getting ever nearer the road and Beinn Chreagach. Alasdair, tremulous from the nearness and vulnerability of his quarry, fired on him again. And again. And then once more, feverishly pushing the rounds into the breach. But on each occasion, there was only the whang as the shot hit a rock or the plumping sound and the flurry of white as it carved through the snow.

Then An Sionnach headed out across a long stretch of unprotected land and Alasdair at last saw his chance of another open shot. Hastily he reached for a bullet but the fingers which scrabbled around his pocket found only an old match and a small ball of twine. To his horror and bitter disappointment, he realised that he had no more ammunition. Well, to hell with it then, I'll take the bugger with my bare hands and the knife. And as this thought ran through his mind, he slipped his hand to the back of his belt and felt the haft of his great knife that lay against his back.

And once again they were away, jogging and panting over the snow in rigid formation. Out across the road and then bending back south-westwards across the slopes and furrows of Beinn Chreagach. And here the puzzling in Alasdair's mind grew denser for the route they were taking pointed in the direction of Cragaig. What had An Sionnach in mind now? Surely the dim bugger knew that he risked being cornered on the cliffs. . . ?

And, imperceptibly at first and then ever faster, Alasdair began to gain on An Sionnach as the latter started to show signs of exhaustion. His left arm hung woodenly at his side and his head rolled as he ran.

Off the slopes of Beinn Chreagach they came and out across the plateau above Cragaig. Now Alasdair was bounding forward, full of an extravagant energy that was fed to him by the growing prospect of revenge for his dead beasts, which lay ripped and tortured only yards away over the lip of the plateau above the sea.

11

THE burn that flowed through the village of Cragaig started its life high on the hills just to the north. It came bubbling and pushing from beneath a slab of cold rock, untiringly driven upwards by hidden forces, to fill a small pool of electric-green mosses. In its turn, the pool spilled over and the water slipped into a rocky channel and the burn itself was born. In that upland hollow where the well lay, the land's life could be seen as the liquid pulsated and pumped out to the surface as if from some broken artery far below. The ground about the well-head was tender and trembling.

Once it left the well and started out over the edge of the pool the water lost the cryptic purity of the inner regions and was quickly joined by drainage from the land, seeping through the peat and carrying with it endless remnants and trophies of the moulting surface. Little specks of rock, minute cast-offs of the plant life, oily brown juices from the black peat earth and all the other manifold forms of detritus were gifted into the sleek waters so that as they grew in volume they also developed in character and appearance.

And the burn grew unexpectedly as countless

other sources found themselves impelled by the contours of the hill to join and mingle with what had started, only a few hundred feet above, as an unambitious trickle. It came bouncing and skipping down the hill, rushing through small-scale gorges of rock and dropping in feathery flutings over sudden falls in the slope until it met the path of another burn that ran seawards from a point to the east. The swollen waters plunged on a while, heading in a northwesterly direction as if intending to pass by the back of Cragaig. But suddenly they ran up against a layer of bed-rock and, unable to force a passage, they turned abruptly through an angle of ninety degrees and set off again to the southwest to pass the lower edge of the village and leap out through the gullet to their salted cousin, the sea.

But at the point where the burn turned in its track before the rock, a deep pool had formed. On the inner side of the bend the water lay sluggish and was rimmed with growths of creamy foam like the head on a glass of beer; while the main flow was thrown swirling and twisting past the sloping outcrop of rock that had barred its path. Opposite the rock, the bank was a steep tongue of dark earth embedded with loose rocks and withered heather roots.

On that afternoon, with the turning-point of the winter only a week or two away, the pool in the burn lay black and menacing against the surrounding snow. Above, the blue sky was already flecked and peppered with the first of the clouds rolling in from the southwest. An uncertain, temperamental wind licked and pulled at the water, kicking up small waves and countercurrents across the pool. The snow, with the day's sun and the dwindling cold, had already taken on the grey stickiness of decline.

And from away over the small plateau to the north of the burn, the figures of the two men came heaving and rolling in exhaustion.

Alasdair was no longer aware of the exhaustion of the extended chase. By now, his eyes were almost constantly on the figure of An Sionnach who ran on, swaying and stumbling like a demented puppet. The land before them was blocked by the hills which stretched sideways out to the very edge of the cliffs. If An Sionnach tried to escape over the side of the hills in the direction of his house, Alasdair was sure of catching him for the wounded man would be slow in the climb.

But even as he eyed the hills, Alasdair caught sight of a woman in a dark blue dress floundering through the snow down the side of a corrie, moving jerkily as if caught in a sticky paste. Several times she fell but rose to her feet with a desperate urgency and hurried on. She, too, was converging on An Sionnach's course. She came out on to the flatter ground just as An Sionnach dipped and vanished into the dent in the land where the burn ran. A few seconds later she had joined him.

Alasdair slowed his pace, puzzled by the sudden
appearance of An Sionnach's woman and by the
fact that they now both lay hidden from view.
What was she after doing? And how the hell had
she known that her man was to be there? For
sure, she might have been out on the hills looking
for him but there was something gey queer in the
timing of it. . . . Had there been some plan all the
time. . .?

As he came up the back of the rise that over-
hung the burn, Alasdair hesitated. While he and
An Sionnach had been skirmishing in the hills,
the thought of the kill had been only too simple.
A savage man treated with savagery. But now the
appearance of the woman and the memories that
she brought with her jolted him into doubt. It
was with a touch of shyness in his eyes that he
came over the rise and looked down on the burn.

Below him lay the pool with its dark waters.
On the other bank, a few yards up the slope,
stood An Sionnach and the woman. She had her
back to Alasdair and was talking vehemently to
her man. As Alasdair appeared, An Sionnach
put his hand on the woman's shoulder and
slowly pushed her aside. She turned and, seeing
Alasdair, backed nervously away from An Sionnach.

An Sionnach. Beneath his thin dusty eyebrows
his eyes, red-rimmed, flickered coldly. Skin of
sickly paleness. Thin, crimped hair the colour of
malt whisky. In his middle thirties, lightly built

but wiry. His right hand grasping the upper part of his other arm where the sweater was stained with blood below a makeshift tourniquet. Alasdair felt himself being drawn, like a bird before a snake, by the eyes that were set like small pebbles in the haggard features. The lips of the man were pressed tight together in a purplewhite stroke.

Alasdair broke free for a moment and glanced over to the woman. She stood tense, her hands locked together over her stomach, her body tilted slightly forwards, her eyes moving from one man to the other. She was chewing at her lower lip. All three of them were breathing heavily. And below them the rustling and quaking of the burn.

The three figures stood motionless, a triangle of forces. The new wind was twisting about, running around them and writing strange signs on the surface of the pool. Time and the beckoning future were trying to press them forward. But they were locked by indecision, each of the men no longer quite sure of himself, frightened of taking the irreversible first step that would push the last lap of the chase into action; while the woman hung poised, not knowing how to halt what she feared was coming. A flock of gulls, screeching, were driving a marauding hoodie away across the hill.

Then, almost involuntarily, out of the depths of his trance, Alasdair takes a step forward and the triangle is released. An Sionnach tenses, prepares himself, casts his eyes around in calculation. But it is the woman who breaks loose and cries out in a voice wound tight with panic.

'Away Alasdair! Away for Christ's sake! He'll be for the killing of ye. He canne bear to hear of ye, ye and your good life, himself so unthanking and jealous. Leave now, for as sure as God is God, he'll be for having ye!' Both men look at her. Alasdair sees her chest heaving, her whole face wrought with anxiety. An Sionnach turns and snaps at her to hold her tongue.

In Alasdair's mind the churning forces start to slow down. He looks out across the water to An Sionnach and sees in the man's still-born eyes and the set of his jaw, the undisguisable look of hatred. He feels puzzled. How can a man feel jealous of him to the point of hatred? He who has lived his years without claiming anything from the world. For him there has been his work to do and an undemonstrative joy when it was done. And then the leisure to rest and think. Nothing more. He who has felt ill of no man; indeed, has known no man well enough to feel ill of him. What did he know of others that could tempt him, could arouse feelings of envy or jealousy? Alasdair Mór was a man apart.

And as he looked across at the face of the man, he felt pity for him. Pity that the business of living should have bent a man into such a pointless state. Perhaps, Alasdair thought to himself, he's no finding it so easy starting up here on the island. Perhaps the life was easier where he came from. If, perhaps, he were to lend the man a hand from time to time. . . . But then, with a twist of his memory as he thought back to the problems of a crofter's life, he recalled his animals. In the byre at Cragaig. Dead. Mutilated. By the man before him. And even as he felt the fury surging again in his head, he spoke with a weighty, anguished slowness.

'Oh, by Christ, ye bad bugger, Sionnach!' And as this simple but heartfelt expression of the pain within him rolled onwards into a maddened groan, Alasdair plucked the knife from his belt and started down the slippery rocks to the pool.

At his first movement, the scene came alive. An Sionnach spun round and made off up the slope. The woman sprang forward and shrieked Alasdair's name in a final attempt to stop the bloodshed; but Alasdair was already beyond reach. He half ran, half skidded down the rocks and waded into the pool. Only when he was most of the way across, with the water up to his waist, did he look up for An Sionnach. And he saw that An Sionnach had not been trying to escape at all when he had turned but had only gone a few yards higher up the slope. He was now on his back in the snow, bracing himself against the ground while his feet kicked and heaved at an enormous oblong rock. And in the moment that he looked up, Alasdair knew what was going to happen. He halted, tried to turn or move aside but the stones on the bed of the burn were treacherous with slime and he almost went down. And as he came up, he heard the woman cry out a warning. With a final thrust and an explosive grunt An Sionnach had dislodged the rock. It hung, undecided, for a second and then broke away leaving a peat-black hole in the snow behind it. Its first moment of descent was slow and cumbersome but then, in its next revolution, it gathered speed and was thundering downwards crushing everything before it. Alasdair stood rooted to the spot.

The rock struck a ledge just above the pool, kicked and took to the air. Alasdair's arms went up, dropping the knife, and his hands reached out like a child trying to catch a ball, but the rock caught him full on the chest and he went sideways and backwards into the pool beneath it. A tremendous plumping sound as man and rock broke the surface, followed quickly by a pillar of spray. Waves ran out and returned and collided across the pool.

With a howl of pain Alasdair's head broke the surface near the edge of the pool. But the cry was cut short as his rising head whipped back in the contortions of pain and suffocation and struck a boulder behind him. For a few seconds his head slumped forward in unconsciousness. The waves subsided to show Alasdair's body wedged between two stones just below the surface and the vast rock lying across his knees. His cap was drifting away across the pool.

Alasdair began to stir.

'Oh. . . ! my legs!' The groan rose and fled across the bubblings of the burn. He lay there, propped by the wedging stones, the water lapping round his chest, his face creased by the rigours of pain.

'Oh, dear God!' The woman's voice broke into the wavering of tears and she ran forward to the pool.

'Leave him be!' An Sionnach's command was a rasp of anger. For a moment the woman froze in terror under his narrowed eyes, but then her distraught face suddenly composed itself and hardened, her weeping put aside. Through teeth—oh the teeth!—bared in fury, her answer was a hiss of loathing.

'God damn ye!' And with that she rushed towards Alasdair.

For a man with two bullet wounds in his arm, An Sionnach moved with surprising speed. He sprang down the slope and reached the water just as the woman was wading into the pool. He hurled himself from the bank and caught her about the shoulders in mid-flight. The force of the impact was such that they both went down into the middle of the pool in a tangle of limbs and a wild thrashing. It was she who rose to the surface first, punching upwards for air, spluttering and gasping, her hair matted across her face. But An

Sionnach had never loosened his grip on her
and when he came up he had her tight by the
arm.

He shook himself like a dog and holding the
woman's arm, dragged her weeping and subdued
out of the pool. On the bank they both stood
fighting for breath, An Sionnach clutching at his
wounded arm. The woman looked over at Alasdair,
who hardly noticed what was going on, and then
turning back to An Sionnach, she said pleadingly
through her tears:

'Ye canne just leave him there!'

'Ach yon stone'll keep the bugger warm the
night. Come now as I say.' And with that he
grips her arm and turns her away towards home.
Unwillingly she goes, twisting her head round to
see, through the distortion of her tears, the
strangely ludicrous sight of the man sitting in
the water. But An Sionnach keeps pushing her on
through the snow and it is not long before their
steps take them round the edge of the hill and out
towards the point of Rudha na Leap.

The pain was excruciating. The rock that had
knocked him backwards into the water had
landed across his knees, breaking the bones of
his legs and cutting deep into the flesh. Had it
fallen slightly higher on his legs he might have
managed to move it but as it was, every attempt
that he made to shift it squeezed a gasp of
agony from his throat. And slowly the coldness of
the waters began to creep through him, chilling

him to his very guts and bringing with it a numbing apathy to his mind.

The sun was beginning to head down over the line of the Cragaig cliffs. Its rays came obliquely from out over the sea, glancing off both the snow and the water of the burn so that Alasdair found himself facing into a silent screen of light.

For a while he lay there moaning gently, turning his head this way and that, trying to hide from the pain and the steady dazzle of the sun. A couple of times, in sudden fits of despair, he began to reach forward for the rock. But he was halted sharply as his body bucked with pain and he slumped back in exhaustion, his face crumpling into the knottings of a squalling child, the black stubble on his chin standing out clearly against the whiteness of his skin. Each moment, the sun was gathering speed in its descent.

Leave now! Leave now! The woman's cry echoed backwards and forwards across his consciousness. Aye, she was right. For the forty-five years of his life and more the land had turned all its forces against Alasdair and his family. The people had dug themselves in against storm and rain, had built themselves sturdy refuges in protection, had managed to squeeze a bare living out of the infertile earth and the murderous sea. Men had drowned, old folk had collapsed beneath the meagreness of the diet, children had turned away in despair to the ease of the mainland towns. Only a few had held on, surviving from year to year through an inborn hardiness and the pig-headed ties of habit. Men born in Cragaig had seen each other—as they had seen their parents and grandparents before them—slowly succumbing to the unhurried ravages of the headland life that pinched and pressed at mind and body in an unending series of aggression. Sometimes they were cheered by days of sun and warmth, but this was only a cruel taunting for almost immediately the wind and rains returned in new strength to lambaste them. And the rain would be followed by gales; the gales by frost; the frost by snow; the snow by rain. Families found their roofs blown off their houses, their boats wrecked in storms, their kale-yard turned into a morass or frozen to ridges of iron, their cattle decimated by disease, their bairns scraggy from undernourishment—and still they stayed. They found time to laugh and joke and to smother the pains of their lives—which they had almost ceased to notice—with the melancholic elations of their ceilidhs. For those many years they had pressed on with a strange joy in this existence of suffering, never blaming one of the younger people for leaving, never bending below the grief of a sudden death, but holding themselves rigidly towards the future, a future which, without doubt, would bring them no relief. This was their land, an inheritance which could not be traded for anything else. If they went under, then the village must go with them.

But in the years preceding Alasdair's birth, the backbone of the community had been broken. The drift had started. It seemed to Alasdair that the whole life of the village had been handed into his keeping, invested in his trust. And he found in this thankless task a true labour of love. Even when he cursed at the weather and the misfortunes of his existence, it was with an amorous chaffing, with the indulgence of deep-seated affection. Never once had he had a moment's doubt about his home.

And so, for all those years, he had found himself standing alone, without support or relief, against the petulance and fury of the land. Previously, the families at Cragaig had been bound together in an unspoken alliance against the forces that would push them off the headland and they had drawn strength from the knowledge that others suffered and believed with them. But for Alasdair it was different. It was through a cheerless, immutable faith that he stood his ground, tying himself gradually tighter to the lonely life as he became ever warier of an outside world he did not know. But the recent years had seen him begin to bend under the strain of his solitude and poverty. He had tightened his belt and turned his mind away from the prospect of approaching old age.

As he lay in the water, gripped by the spasms of pain from his shattered legs, Alasdair saw the culminating stages of this battle between his people and the land. People going, people dying, walls falling, weeds growing: until, at last, Alasdair had been cornered alone. And he saw An Sionnach, not as a hard and vicious neighbour, but as an agent. An agent sent to deliver the final blow.

Aye, she was right, the woman. There was no peace on the headland for the folk of Cragaig. I'd be best away, she said . . . aye, well, there might be truth enough in that. And the village would see no more suffering. Aye, she was right enough, An Sionnach's woman. . . . An Sionnach. A queer one there. The bugger would no have me at Cragaig either. Well, that's the way with folk. Like Wee Jamie would no have me sit next to him that time at school. . . . But yon woman's a fine lassy. I'd gey like to see her away from yon man of hers. . . . But they'll no have me away. My home's my home and I'll no leave it. . . .

Alasdair Mór had decided. The matter was resolved. The man's love was truly unassailable: right or wrong in the terms of the passing world, he was finally proved incapable of breaking faith. In this hour of defeat, his innocence never left him. And so it was that, unknown to him, the world became his.

And as the first strains of delirium begin to float into Alasdair's mind, the sun falls behind the level of the cliffs and a damp chill settles on the land. Slowly the sky covers over with the clouds and beneath this dull canopy a premature darkness falls. About an hour after sunset, the surface of the pool begins to prickle with drops of rain. At first, only a few fecund drops that strike the waters with an oily sound; but soon the rain increases and a light brushwork of drizzle is swept again and again across the countryside. The thaw has begun.

For a while, the drizzle stops and a young stag, not scenting the man in the water, comes down to the pool to drink, but a quiet groan over to its right sends it bounding in terror back to the safety of the hills. Several times during the early hours of the night, animals are scared away from the water by disjointed mumblings from out of the dark.

Close on midnight, a short-eared owl, curving its flight round over the burn senses something below it. It turns and comes back low but swings away violently and hurries off at the sudden sound of splashing and a man's voice.

'Aye, well I'd best be away home the now. I'll need to be seeing to the cow.' A short laugh followed by a shaking gasp of pain.

That night the cold waters of the burn and the massive rock across his legs helped Alasdair Mór hold to his resolution.